"What's wrong with Shy Boots?" Sam blurted.

Jen said, "He won't get up."

"See for yourself," Ryan said, walking closer to the box stall.

The chocolate-brown colt with his hip blanket of white spots wasn't unconscious. His eyes were open, but there was no luster beyond those impossibly long eyelashes.

Listless and still, he watched the humans stare down at him.

Ryan slipped inside the stall and squatted beside Shy Boots. His only movement was a slight flinch away from the stroking of Ryan's hand against his dark velvety neck.

Ryan was the sort of guy who tried to hide his emotions, but Sam could tell his love for the Appaloosa foal made him anxious as a father. Ryan was so concerned for his colt, he didn't care about his appearance, and Sam wanted to pat him on the back.

Read all the books about the

Phantom Stallion

Phantom Stallion

∽ 21 ∽
Dawn Runner

TERRI FARLEY

AVON BOOKS

An Imprint of HarperCollins*Publishers*

Library of Congress Catalog Card Number: 2005906564
ISBN-10: 0-06-081538-8 — ISBN-13: 978-0-06-081538-7

❖

First Avon edition, 2006

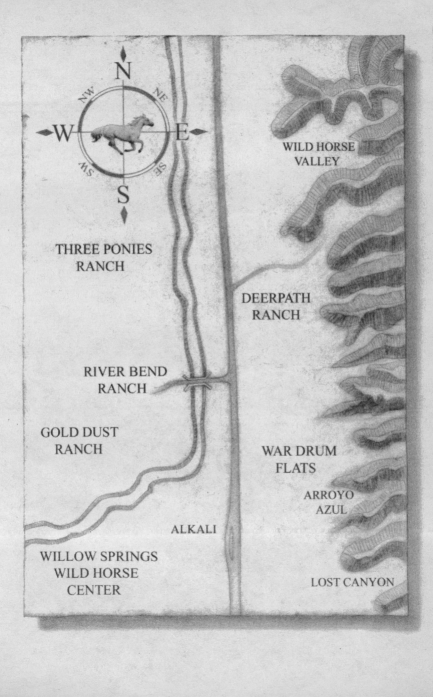

Chapter One ❧

Glossy Shetland ponies crowded together in the late afternoon shade of cottonwood trees. Standing head to tail, they whisked breezes over each other's faces as if nothing were wrong.

For them, nothing was, but Samantha Forster was worried. How could something she'd wished for bring bad luck to the wild horses she loved?

The early September sun sizzled against Sam's back. Summer hadn't ended just because it was the first day of school.

She glanced toward the mansion sitting atop the man-made hill overlooking Gold Dust Ranch. The oversized house was air-conditioned and after the long walk from the school bus stop to visit her best friend, that refrigerated air would feel wonderful.

But her best friend lived in the foreman's house, not the mansion. Sam knew she was more likely to receive an invitation from the ponies, to share their irrigated emerald pasture, than one into Linc Slocum's giant pillared house.

She'd worn a knit shirt Gram had called adobe red, and a denim skirt, because Gram and Brynna, her stepmother, had ganged up on her until she'd accepted their claim that she only had one chance to make a good impression on her teachers during this first week of school. But the shirt was too warm for the sunny afternoon, especially when she was carrying two sets of books.

Fretting over the temperature made a nice change from replaying last night's phone call.

Forget about the heat and the phone call, Sam told herself as she knocked at the front door of the small foreman's house near Gold Dust Ranch's front gates. But she couldn't.

At first she'd been so excited. Pam O'Malley, her best friend from San Francisco, was coming to Nevada. Right this minute, Pam and her mom should be driving their camper from the city to Lost Canyon. Sam was excited to see Pam again and she couldn't wait for her old best friend to meet her new one, but then Pam had announced the reason for their trip.

"My mom has a grant to study mythological horses and write a paper about them," Pam had explained.

"She's going to investigate the wild horses around your area, and focus on stories of some legendary stallion."

The only legendary stallion in northern Nevada was the Phantom. Sam knew that as well as she knew the mustang's safety depended on staying hidden, not being put under a magnifying glass.

Sam knocked a second time, then fluttered the neck of her shirt for coolness while she waited for Jennifer Kenworthy, her best friend in the entire world, to let her in out of the sun. Level-headed Jen would help her figure out what to do about Pam and her mother. Jen's passion was complex mathematics, and she loved solving intricate problems of any kind.

But Sam didn't have time to announce her news.

"Stay out," Jen said as soon as she saw Sam.

She didn't sound angry, just firm as she slipped past the screen door to come outside.

Jen's white-blond braids were pinned haphazardly atop her head and her arm moved a little stiffly as it brushed aside the day's homework Sam carried with her.

A week ago, an attack by a range bull had shattered one of Jen's ribs. According to her parents, Jen wasn't well enough yet to return to school, so Sam had brought her new books to her.

With her torso still wrapped in bandages for protection, Jen stepped gingerly off the porch. Sam stepped back to let Jen ease past.

"What's up?" Sam asked.

"Nothing that'll make you happy," Jen said as she led the way across the silently baking ranch yard.

Sam felt her worry double.

As she left the stack of books and homework on the porch, she wondered if Jen's parents had decided their daughter should go back to being homeschooled instead of attending Darton High.

No, a silent voice wailed in Sam's head, but she just crossed her fingers and hoped not. Since Jen's accident, the idea had been under discussion. The last Sam had heard, though, Jen's parents were still locked in disagreement.

"C'mon," Jen said, looking back over her shoulder. "I want you to look at something."

With a sigh of relief, Sam followed. You couldn't look at a decision.

As she fell into step beside her friend, Sam almost blurted out her worries over Pam, but she knew she should be considerate first.

"How does your rib feel?" Sam asked.

"Like the broken ends of that bone are still grating together under my skin," Jen grumbled. "And don't get me started on wearing layers of protective bandages during a heat wave."

Then Jen gave a lopsided grin, probably so Sam wouldn't think she was whining.

Sam shuddered. Heat and sweat she could tolerate, but she winced at her friend's pain. When she opened her mouth to sympathize, Jen stopped her.

"Talking about it is a waste of time."

"Right," Sam said, then turned her head so Jen wouldn't see her smile.

Jen's injury hadn't smothered her take-charge attitude.

"What are you going to show me?" Sam asked. Despite everything, excitement bounced up in her when she noticed they were headed for Gold Dust Ranch's modern barn. The barn meant horses.

"No hints," Jen muttered. "I want your honest assessment. Maybe Ryan and I are overreacting."

Sam took a deep breath. Telling Jen about Pam's visit would have to wait.

Ryan Slocum, whose father owned the Gold Dust Ranch, was new to Nevada, and he sometimes misunderstood the Western way of things. But Jen had been born on this ranch. If Sam added all Jen's experience to the fact that she was a science and math whiz who insisted on a logical explanation for everything, the chances that Jen was overreacting were pretty small.

Sam squinted and blinked as she passed from the glaring sunlight into the dim barn. Before her eyes accustomed themselves to the change, Jen shushed her.

"Wha—?" Sam managed before she made out the index finger Jen had raised to her lips, then pointed.

Sam looked toward the barn's biggest box stall, but it was empty.

The quiet only lasted a second.

Ryan Slocum's voice sliced through it. Squinting her dazzled eyes, Sam made him out, standing near a wall-mounted telephone.

"Pardon me," he said, to whoever listened on the other end of the line, but he didn't sound apologetic. "I don't mean to be too direct, but I've been waiting—no, it's not an emergency. Not exactly. You see, this is my second call to Dr. Scott and I've yet to hear . . ."

Sam stiffened. Dr. Scott was the nearest veterinarian. If Ryan had phoned the vet twice, something must be seriously wrong. And it must be about Shy Boots, the colt Ryan loved.

"Yes, actually, I've been concerned for several days," Ryan continued. "However, I've driven the distance between—" Ryan's lecturing tone broke off and he flinched. "Oh, I see, a pet tortoise hit by a car. That's dreadful." Ryan sighed. "Well then, I suppose there's nothing to do except wait. You've been quite helpful," Ryan added, and then he hung up and turned toward Sam.

"What's wrong with Shy Boots?" Sam blurted.

Seeing that her plan for an impartial evaluation was doomed, Jen said, "He won't get up."

"Won't or can't?" Sam asked. Although she'd never seen the problem, she'd heard of "cast" horses who got wedged in weird positions in their stalls and couldn't gather themselves to rise.

"See for yourself," Ryan said, walking closer to the box stall.

It turned out not to be empty. When Sam peered inside and saw the Appaloosa foal lying flat, she instantly forgot the sunshine outside. In here, it might as well be November.

The chocolate-brown colt with his hip blanket of white spots wasn't unconscious. His eyes were open, but there was no luster beyond those impossibly long eyelashes.

Listless and still, he watched the humans stare down at him.

Ryan slipped inside the stall and squatted beside Shy Boots. The colt seemed limp. His only movement was a slight flinch away from the stroking of Ryan's hand against his dark, velvety neck.

Ryan was the sort of guy who tried to hide his emotions, but Sam could tell his love for the Appaloosa foal made him as anxious as a father.

He didn't even look like himself. His dark hair was disheveled. His pressed khaki pants were smeared with—nope, she wasn't seeing things—a little horse manure.

Sam rarely understood what Jen saw in Ryan Slocum, her almost-boyfriend.

Right now, though, Ryan was so concerned about his colt, he didn't care about his appearance, and Sam wanted to pat him on the back.

"Boots won't leave his stall and his appetite has slacked off dramatically," Ryan said without looking up at Sam.

"Ryan's checked for a temperature," Jen added,

"but the thermometer reads right at one hundred degrees." Jen gave Sam an owlish glance. "And that's normal."

"Okay," Sam said. "Could he have hurt himself? Just pulled a tendon and be feeling crummy?"

"There's no sign of trauma or swelling." Jen bit her lip. Jen planned to study veterinary medicine in college and she'd already started looking at animals as patients. Above the nosepiece of her glasses, her frown deepened. "I've thought of West Nile virus, but I can't find any insect bite and I'm not up on all the symptoms—"

"Jen," Sam interrupted. "Why don't we wait for the vet?"

"It could be a while, and I can't even enjoy the satisfaction of feeling angry. Not without being a brute," Ryan said. "You heard what I said about the tortoise being backed over by a car?"

The girls nodded, grimacing.

"I'm sure Boots is fine," Jen said, trying to sound casual. "But the poor little guy's been through so much."

Sam took a deep breath, and when she exhaled, she felt no relief. Jen was right.

Sired by a rogue stallion named Diablo and mothered by Hotspot, a young mare who'd escaped before she could become the cornerstone of Gold Dust Ranch's Appaloosa breeding program, Shy Boots had been unwanted before he was even born.

Soon after the mare and foal had survived a difficult birth, Linc Slocum had tried to wean Shy Boots early.

That was one of the rare times when Ryan, whose heart had been won by the two horses, had stood up to his father. Ryan had objected to the early separation, and so had Hotspot. Although she'd been purchased solely as a broodmare, Hotspot had refused to mate with a stallion whose high-priced bloodlines matched her own.

Just days later, Ryan had overheard Linc's plan to solve the problem by destroying Hotspot's "mongrel" foal.

Before that could happen, the horses had been stolen, then separated. Luckily, the inept thief hadn't gotten very far with the horses. Hotspot had escaped and joined the Phantom's herd and Shy Boots had been found at a petting zoo, where he'd been adopted by a burro foster mother. But that arrangement had been temporary.

Now, with Hotspot still out on the range, the colt was alone again.

Jen was right. The little guy had been through a lot.

"Maybe he's just tired and overwhelmed," Sam suggested.

"He's not eating, even though I offer him the bottle all the time, now," Ryan said. Something in his tone sounded a little guilty, and Sam could guess why.

When Jen had been in the hospital, Ryan had spent hours driving back and forth to Darton. Then he sat in a chair at her beside, talking. Jen had appreciated his company, but who had fed Shy Boots?

Ryan was an excellent rider, but had he ever been responsible for the daily care of his own horse? In England, there had been grooms and trainers to monitor his horses' health. Did he know foals needed frequent feeding, even when humans thought they had more important things to do?

Before she could bring up the touchy subject, they all heard a faint mechanical *whirr*, then a *clang* as the iron gates to Gold Dust Ranch opened and closed.

From his bed of straw, Shy Boots' dark ears twitched, picking up the sound of an approaching truck.

"That will be Dr. Scott," Ryan said, and Sam saw him return to being his usual self.

With brisk movements, he stood, brushed at his soiled pants, and left the stall.

He tossed back his dark hair and shed the worry that had bowed him over the foal. As Ryan made his way toward the vet, his manner said he wasn't the sort of guy who liked to be kept waiting.

Chapter Two ∾

*A*pparently Ryan had calmed down under Dr. Scott's quiet questioning, because he leaned casually against the barn wall, pretending to be unconcerned as the vet examined Shy Boots.

The vet lifted the Appaloosa, steadied him on his faintly striped hooves, and coaxed him into a paddock outside the barn. But the open space didn't tempt the colt to cavort in circles or nibble dandelions. In fact, he didn't do much of anything.

He'd changed a lot since the day Ryan had brought him over to play with her filly Tempest, Sam thought. Then, he'd bucked in high spirits. He'd chased and played hide-and-seek behind his mother. Now, Shy Boots turned his head away from the humans and stared toward the range as if he knew where his mother had gone.

"Clinically, we'd diagnose his condition as 'failure to thrive,'" Dr. Scott announced finally.

"I guess I'll need to talk with that woman Patty," Ryan snapped. "Her precious burro Mistress Mayhem," he pronounced the name almost scornfully, "is needed here, where she can take care of Boots."

Ryan's attitude had just changed again. Since Sam had arrived, he'd gone from concerned, to irritated, to casual, and back to irritated. She and Jen knew he loved Shy Boots. Dr. Scott probably knew, too. So why did Ryan try to cover it up?

"If Patty didn't want to sell her burro two weeks ago, she won't want to now," Jen told him. "Even if she loaned Mistress Mayhem to you, Patty would eventually want her back. Then Boots would lose her twice."

"Right," Ryan said curtly.

They faced the vet, waiting for his solution to the problem.

Dr. Scott pushed his black-rimmed glasses up with the back of one hand. He looked thoughtful. Sam knew he was about to come up with something, but the vet was testing Ryan's patience.

"Should I try to find his real mother?" Ryan demanded.

Dr. Scott must have been used to people turning emotional over their animals, because he pretty much ignored Ryan and spoke slowly as he worked through the colt's situation.

"If Shy Boots were a human child—given his bumpy start—I'd say you'd be looking at trouble on down the line. But horses tend to bounce back from trouble. Once we clear up his physical problems, we'll probably see a big improvement."

"What are his physical problems?" Ryan asked.

"I'm guessing he has an ulcer," Dr. Scott said.

"Guessing?" Fear made Ryan's voice louder. "But you're not sure?"

The vet shrugged. "We could test him, but I'd rather not add to his stress. Ulcer treatment will do him good no matter what's wrong."

An ulcer? Sam stared at Shy Boots. Didn't people in high-pressure jobs, like heads of corporations or brain surgeons, get ulcers?

Sam moved her hands against her arms as if she were rubbing away a chill. Poor little horse.

This time Ryan didn't snap at the vet. When he did speak, his British accent seemed stronger than usual. "Because he feels abandoned, d'you think?"

"I can't read his mind," Dr. Scott admitted. "But it's probably more physical than emotional. In the wild, horses spend almost all their waking hours grazing, then moving around looking for more grass, and grazing some more. His whole digestive system," the vet said, nodding at Shy Boots, "is designed for a life of constant intake and exercise."

When Ryan stayed quiet, the vet added, "Eat. Move. Eat again and move on to look for food, then eat some more."

"I understood," Ryan told him. "In fact, I was just thinking about his confinement and," Ryan's cheeks flushed slightly, "his eating schedule." He shook his head. Then his hands spread wide as something else occurred to him. "But many horses are kept in stalls and fed on a schedule."

"And lots of 'em have ulcers," Dr. Scott said. "I read a study not long ago that said plenty of race-horses and performance horses have ulcers, and so do most orphaned foals."

"Does he count as an orphan?" Sam asked.

"Yes and no," Dr. Scott said. "Yes, because he can't nurse every hour, getting nutrition the minute he needs it. No, because he was with his mother right after birth. In those first six to twelve hours, nursing babies don't get milk—"

"They get colostrum," Jen said proudly.

Ryan murmured in agreement.

"That's right," Dr. Scott said.

Sam raised her hand as if she were in class. "Excuse me. Since I'm the only one who doesn't know what col—whatever—is, could someone please tell me?"

"Colostrum is a liquid that's like fifty-fifty sugar and antibodies," Jen explained.

"Something like that," Dr. Scott agreed, smiling at

Jen's knowledge. "But the main thing is, it helps young animals fight off disease."

"Fine then," Ryan said. He sounded as if he were brushing aside his earlier worry.

"However," Dr. Scott said in a cautioning tone, "first-time mothers don't always give their young enough of it, and he's reached the age when the positive effects start wearing off." In the sudden silence, they all stared at the vulnerable colt. "But I don't think we need to worry about that. My advice—" Dr. Scott paused to look at Ryan.

"Yes, please," Ryan urged.

"—is to kill two birds with one stone. Put him on open pasture with another horse so he can do what horses do, moving around at will, nibbling at grass, staring at butterflies, and napping. He'll avoid long periods of fasting—that's tough on his tummy—and he'll be feeding in the proper position, with his head down and throat"—Dr. Scott's hand moved up his own neck—"extended. That'll take care of his physical need for exercise and his emotional need for company."

"Just a moment," Ryan protested, then looked sort of sheepish. "I do spend quite a good deal of time with him."

"I meant equine company," the vet said. "And it would be best, 'til he shakes off his blues, if you limited human contact."

"Why is that?" Jen asked.

"Sometimes it helps to let creatures return, as much as possible, to what they've been doing for millions of years," Dr. Scott said. Then he shrugged, adding, "And it's an easy step to try first."

Ryan's arms crossed hard across his middle. He looked cold-eyed and determined. He wanted to reject the idea of not spending time with the lonely colt, and Sam understood.

"But Shy Boots has imprinted on Ryan," Sam said, remembering the days Ryan had refused to leave Hotspot and her colt. "Won't that be hard for him?"

"Maybe at first," Dr. Scott conceded, "but he needs the company of other horses, needs to learn what they do and how they respond to their world, if he's not going to be a misfit."

Ryan exhaled and his arms dropped to his sides. "Clearly, that's not what I want." He looked away from the vet and stared toward the pastures. "Now," he said, and cleared his throat loudly, "our next chore is to select the perfect companion."

"I already know," Jen said.

"Not your Silly," Ryan protested, referring to Silk Stockings, Jen's beautiful but skittish palomino mare.

"No, not my Silly." Jen stuck her tongue out at him. It was such an uncharacteristically childish gesture that Sam, Ryan, and even Dr. Scott laughed.

When Jen pointed to a pasture across the ranch,

indicating the graceful sorrel grazing closest to them, Sam followed her gesture. But she wasn't prepared when Jen said, "Princess Kitty."

Chills rained down Sam's arms.

Princess Kitty had once lived at River Bend Ranch. Sam's ranch. The mare had been sold to the Kenworthys right after Sam's accident because . . . Sam's next breath caught, and she drew another one, despite the tightness in her chest. Because Dad couldn't stand to look at Princess Kitty since she'd given birth to the horse who'd injured Sam. Princess Kitty was the Phantom's mother.

So why hadn't Dad sold Smoke, too? Dad's gray mustang had been the Phantom's father. Sam shook her head. Why should she try to unravel Dad's emotions, when she couldn't even figure out her own?

Right now, for instance, she felt totally protective of the mare as Dr. Scott and Ryan discussed her suitability as a companion for Shy Boots.

"She's a pretty thing," Ryan said, looking the horse over with considering eyes. "And I have heard them call to one another in sort of a conversational way."

"Some people believe in something called breed recognition," Dr. Scott said, "and I'd have to say that Kitty's conformation is pretty close to Hotspot's."

Sam had never noticed before, but the vet was right. Although Princess Kitty was probably a full hand shorter than Hotspot, she had the same fine-legged, lean-bodied running Quarter Horse body.

"Will she know how to conduct herself around a foal, though?" Ryan asked. "That's rather critical. If she should get short-tempered around Shy Boots—"

"She's had a foal," Sam interrupted. "She's the Phantom's mother."

Dr. Scott gave a surprised sound and tilted his head.

"You don't say?" Ryan said, incredulously. "Your fabled silver stallion has a little brown hen of a mother?"

"Ryan!" Jen wailed, and despite her bandages, she swatted him on the shoulder.

"I'm joking," he assured her as he stepped out of reach. "Didn't I just say she was pretty?"

But another thought made Jen turn toward Sam.

"Sam," Jen said as if she'd suddenly remembered something, "she had another foal, too."

"She did?" Sam yelped.

Her imagination sprang into action. She pictured a half-brother or sister to the Phantom, a silver shadow to run alongside him on the range.

"Where is he?" Sam blurted. "Or she?"

"Sold," Jen said in gloomy certainty. "Gone away—somewhere . . ." Jen shrugged. "Kitty foaled when we were trying to hold onto the ranch by selling off everything that would bring us a dollar." Jen blushed under Ryan's stare. "It didn't work, of course, and Kitty went as part of the ranch when we sold it."

"But what about the foal? Who bought her? Or him?" Sam asked.

"My parents might remember, but I don't. That year was . . ." Jen paused, searching for the right word. When she settled on one, Sam would bet it didn't come close to describing the despair of losing a ranch you'd worked and sacrificed for. "It was kind of crazy around here. I just remember one day there was this little baby horse with floppy ears and the next day there wasn't."

Floppy ears? Sam thought of her beautiful ivory stallion with pricked ears delicate as a desert Arabian's, but before she could grill Jen for more details, her friend added, "She was in foal a third time, too, to Sundance, but not for long."

"What happened?" Sam asked.

"I don't know," Jen admitted.

"It just happens that way sometimes," Dr. Scott said. "I wasn't here, of course, but there could've been a serious birth defect in the foal or, if things were as stressful in her environment as Jen says, Princess Kitty might have just miscarried."

In the moment of quiet, Sam realized this was her chance to get to know the Phantom's mother. She'd bring Jen her homework every day and check on Shy Boots and Princess Kitty at the same time.

But Ryan's thoughts had veered in another direction.

"If I'm going to limit Boots's human contact, I

might as well go out and find his mother straight away," Ryan said. "It will be safer than letting BLM bring her in, herding her with helicopters, running her over rough terrain with dozens of other horses."

Ryan's musing expression cleared as he shot a quick glance at Sam.

"You're right," Sam told him. Just because Brynna, her stepmother, worked for the Bureau of Land Management didn't mean she was blind to the dangers of horses running, frightened and full-out.

"Someone will still need to keep an eye on him," Dr. Scott said, nodding toward Shy Boots.

"If they both came to River Bend, Gram would be there during the day and I could work with them after school." Sam's words rushed out in excitement. "That would be incredibly cool. Boots could play with Tempest again and I bet Dark Sunshine would . . ." Sam's voice trailed off as she wondered. "Well, she got along great with Hotspot, so she'd probably do fine with Kitty."

"That mare's still pretty wild," Dr. Scott said, and Sam knew the vet was being generous. Dark Sunshine was beautiful, but she'd been damaged by confinement and abuse.

Before Sam could make excuses for the buckskin mare, Jen interrupted.

"Same problem as before," Jen insisted. "He'd just get settled and then he'd have to be separated from Tempest and Dark Sunshine. Unless Ryan is willing to give you Shy Boots."

"Which, I am not," Ryan put in.

A few minutes' more discussion brought them all to the same conclusion. Jen and her mother Lila would look after Shy Boots while Ryan searched the range for Hotspot.

"That's great," Jen said, then asked the vet, "Is there any reason we can't put Kitty and Boots together right now, in his paddock?"

"Other than the fact that you're weak as a kitten and your mother will have my hide for keeping you out here?" Dr. Scott asked. "Not a one."

"I feel fine," Jen insisted, but Sam noticed her friend was leaning against the corral fence as if she needed it for support. "I've been in the house resting all day. I'm not going back in there until we try this experiment." When she saw the vet hesitate, Jen pressed her advantage. "If I'm going to be supervising these horses, I want to make sure they get off to a good start."

"Fair enough." Dr. Scott sounded resigned, but he still shot a quick look at the house.

"I'll get Kitty," Sam volunteered, before he could change his mind.

She left the others and walked toward the barn. She'd already noticed the mare wore a sand-colored nylon halter, so Sam only grabbed a lead rope and a bucket from the barn. She poured in a scant scoop of grain that would shift around, making a tantalizing sound inside the bucket.

Princess Kitty guessed Sam was coming for her. As Sam opened the pasture gate and slipped inside, the mare's delicate ears pricked in her direction. The sorrel didn't lift her head, but her teeth stopped clipping grass and her brown eyes gazed through her flaxen forelock.

Sam stopped shaking the grain bucket and stood still.

That peekaboo look—more an acknowledgment than a greeting—made Sam's breath catch. Many times, she'd seen the Phantom do the same thing. He let a veil of forelock shield his eyes while he thought things over.

"Hey beauty," Sam said, taking a step closer. "I know your son."

Of course the mare didn't understand. She couldn't. She was an animal, not a human mother, but Princess Kitty's lips left the green grass. Her head rose, and her luminous brown eyes met Sam's.

"He's doing fine," Sam told the mare, "in case you've been wondering."

When the sorrel gave a faint nicker, Sam swallowed hard. *She just smells the grain,* Sam told herself, but she kept talking as she moved closer.

"He has colts of his own now." Silently, Sam scolded herself for the pang of melancholy that tightened her throat.

Sam tried to tell herself it was nonsense. Princess

Kitty had long since forgotten the black colt she'd lost.

"He lives in wonderful, wild places," Sam said as the mare studied the lead rope.

Sam stood close enough now that she could have touched the horse, but she waited. She wouldn't risk a grab. Not quite yet. With the lead rope in one hand and the bucket in the other, she wasn't set up for a quick capture. One wrong move would make Kitty shy. Then, Sam would be trailing the mare all over the pasture. And she'd have an audience for her mistake.

"We're getting this right the first time, girl," Sam said.

She really was a pretty horse. Red-gold, but whereas Ace's coat was red-gold over rich brown, Kitty's was red-gold over copper.

"Let's go see Shy Boots. He could use some company," Sam said.

Princess Kitty's cheek grazed Sam's as she ducked her head, going for the bucket. She didn't draw back when Sam clipped on the lead rope, but she did give a noisy snuffle, making sure she'd searched out all the grain.

Satisfied she'd eaten it all, Kitty walked quietly beside Sam to the gate. Sam was surprised at Kitty's gentleness, but that surprise had barely registered when the mare sighted Shy Boots.

The colt spotted her at the same time. His high-pitched whinny brought a look of alarm into the mare's eyes. Kitty burst from a standstill into a trot and Sam had to jog to keep up.

"Easy," Sam called, but Princess Kitty ignored her, even when Sam gave a tug on the lead rope and scolded, "Slow down."

Princess Kitty's pace stayed the same, but she glanced back over her shoulder to regard Sam with a royal air that seemed to say, "No, *you* keep up."

Sam couldn't help smiling. She wasn't pleased with the mare's defiance, but it was nice to know that even though Princess Kitty was just one of Linc Slocum's many possessions, she ha0dn't lost the pride she'd passed on to her son.

It would do Shy Boots good to spend time with this horse. Ryan could teach him manners while Kitty taught him nerve.

At last, Sam turned Kitty into Shy Boots's paddock.

Sam stood between Jen and Ryan, watching for the horses' reactions to each other.

After ten minutes, Kitty and Shy Boots were still pretending to ignore each other. After twenty minutes, they'd moved a few steps closer together, but they still didn't seem excited.

Ryan said, "Nothing's happening."

"Nothing we can see or hear," Dr. Scott corrected. "But I think they're going to do fine.

"You know, on some big horse ranches, where they have a dozen brood mares and foals in the same pasture, they wean by slowly removing one or two mothers and replacing them with old saddle horse mares."

Sam wanted to protest. Kitty sure didn't fit that description.

"Of course they notice the difference," Dr. Scott said, "but it's a good solution. The older mares comfort the little ones and teach them how to be around other horses."

Thirty minutes after the horses had been together, just as Jen drooped against the fence and looked ready to give in to her weariness, Shy Boots released a heavy sigh.

"Look," Jen said quietly.

The little Appaloosa lowered himself to the grass, then rested his head against his folded legs. He was down, but his whole attitude was different than before, Sam thought. Shy Boots was relaxed enough to close his eyes and doze.

Beside her, Sam heard Ryan sigh, too.

"I'll be on my way," Dr. Scott said quietly. He stretched his linked hands high over his head, rolled his head from side to side, loosening his neck muscles, and grinned. "This is the kind of house call I like best. I didn't even have to take my bag out of the truck."

"Oh," Jen said suddenly, "how did things turn out with your last patient? Ryan said you were tending a tortoise who'd had a bad accident."

Great, Jen, Sam thought. Why bring up a patient who might have died, when Shy Boots had made the vet happy?

But Jen wanted to be a vet when she grew up. She was probably just curious.

"Agnes, the desert tortoise," the vet said, "is another of today's success stories, although her cure was a little more high-tech."

"Surgery?" Jen asked, eyes widening behind her glasses.

Sam wondered how you'd perform surgery beneath the tortoise's shell.

"Epoxy," Dr. Scott corrected.

"You mean glue?" Sam asked.

"Medical-grade glue," Dr. Scott said, nodding. Then, looking excited, he added, "The shell did just what it was supposed to do, protecting Agnes' soft body, and all the tender stuff inside."

From the corner of her eye, Sam saw Ryan rub his hand across his forehead, shading his eyes as he did.

"The shell only had a little crack," Dr. Scott went on. "I squeezed glue in a ring around the crack, layered in tiny fiberglass sheets, and she should be as good as new."

Sam was glad for Agnes and Dr. Scott, but for some reason she couldn't stop staring at Ryan. His lips pulled down into a frown. Maybe he wished someone could mend the crack Shy Boots had put in the shell he'd worn over his feelings and all the "tender stuff inside."

Chapter Three ☙

Ice cubes tinkled as Lila Kenworthy, Jen's mom, placed a pitcher of pink lemonade on the camp table between Sam and Jen.

Lila had dragged the table and three chairs onto the porch of the foreman's house. The girls had collapsed gratefully in the shade.

"This is great. Thank you," Sam said. As she sipped, a red maraschino cherry bumped her lips. Sam would bet Lila had tinted the lemonade pink by adding the cherries and their juice. Gram did the same thing.

Fanning herself with one hand, Lila smiled and settled into the third chair.

Lemonade, the shady porch, and a plan in place to

help Shy Boots would have made this the perfect time to ask Jen what she should do about Pam, except that she caught Jen shooting a quick look toward Ryan. He still lingered by Shy Boots's paddock, but Jen's expression said she'd hoped the third chair was for him.

Lila didn't notice.

"You're welcome, Sam," Lila said. "Thank *you* for walking out here with Jen's schoolwork. Every year I forget how we suffer in the September heat."

"Darton High is air-conditioned," Jen pointed out, and her mother took the hint.

"Honey, I'm working on him," Lila assured her daughter, and Sam knew the *him* was Jen's dad, Jed. "It's only the first day of school and you're still recovering, so be patient." Lila waited for Jen's grumbling agreement, then turned to Sam. "Tell us about your classes, Sam."

"I have P.E. first thing in the morning," Sam said.

"So you'll be finished before it gets hot," Lila said.

"But in December . . ." Jen began.

"I know." Sam rolled her eyes. "And what good is it trying to look nice when I leave home in the morning, if I'm going to be sweaty and gross an hour later?"

"A problem I yearn to have," Jen said, then stared at her mother with such intensity, Sam wasn't sure she should go on. Was she only making Jen feel left out?

"Go ahead, Sam," Lila urged.

"Then I have English, world history, math, and journalism."

Sam was pleased with her recital, until Jen said, "That's only five classes. Don't you have six?"

"Right," Sam said. Mentally, she reviewed her day, numbering classes off on her fingers. She was about to reach for the printed schedule in her backpack when she remembered. "Oh yeah, one semester of Life Skills."

"What's that?" Lila asked.

"One of those retro fifties classes Mrs. Santos is bringing back, hoping they'll make us successful when we move out on our own," Jen said, with emphasis. "I have to take it, too."

Lila drank the rest of her lemonade, plucked a cherry from her glass, and bit it from its stem.

"Let's hope," she said.

Sam rushed on, trying to distract Jen. She didn't want to be in the middle of family bickering, even though Jen and her mom were on the same side.

"In Life Skills, I start with cooking, but then classes rotate," Sam explained. "Next quarter, I'll have sewing or personal finance—"

"Subjects we could handle at home," Lila put in, as she stood.

"—but then second semester, I'll go back to Spanish," Sam said.

"You girls take your time. Sam, just let me know

when, and I'll call your Gram to come pick you up. Drink all you like," Lila said, nodding to the pitcher. "And I'll bring out another glass."

Sam and Jen followed Lila's glance and saw Ryan headed their way, but Jen didn't let her mother escape.

"And how are you feeling about teaching me calculus, Mom?" Jen teased.

"Helpless," Lila said, grinning. "And that's what's going to win this one for us." Lila held up crossed fingers. "Your dad is no better at higher math than I am. You outpaced both of us when you were in sixth grade." Then, just before she left them, Lila used the back of her hand to check the temperature of Jen's forehead. "Don't push yourself, honey."

"I don't have a fever," Jen said, pulling away from her mother's concerned touch. "It's a hundred degrees out here. Everyone's hot."

Lila nodded, unconvinced.

Once the screen door closed behind her mother, Jen moaned, "If I'm not back in school next week, I don't know what I'll do. Maybe die of boredom."

"Or take care of my colt?" Ryan suggested. Hair slicked down and shirt cuffs turned back, he'd clearly made a trip up to the mansion.

Probably, Sam thought, that's where he'd gotten the folder he was carrying, too.

"Sure, I'll take care of Boots," Jen told him. "But my brilliant mind needs stimulation. Every day counts if I'm going to earn a scholarship to Stanford."

Sam was pretty sure Ryan didn't mean his expression to look so indulgent, but it did, as if he were tolerating a child's dream of sliding down a rainbow.

Whatever he meant by it, the smile was brief. Ryan pulled a chair closer, moved the pitcher aside, and opened his folder.

"Maps," Sam said, as he placed the papers side by side, but then she saw they were actually digital photographs of real maps pierced with multicolored pins.

"Photos of maps on my bedroom wall," Ryan said.

Sam looked up at Ryan expectantly.

But Jen didn't wait for him to explain. Head tilted to one side, she squinted, studied the photos, then said, "You've been thinking about this for a while."

"Yes," he said.

"About what?" Sam asked.

She knew she wasn't dumb. Her grades and standardized test scores said her intelligence was above average, but sometimes, it was hard having a best friend who was brilliant.

"Dr. Scott's diagnosis wasn't what convinced Ryan to try to find Hotspot," Jen told Sam.

"It did, but it wasn't the only thing," Ryan admitted. "I'd already been considering it. What rational person wouldn't want to get back something that's his?"

His defensive tone made Sam look at Jen, but her friend's expression was carefully blank.

Get back *some*thing. *He must mean Hotspot,* Sam thought.

"Of course, my father thinks it's a poor idea. Still, he agreed to let me use Sky Ranger to stalk the herd, even though he's tried unsuccessfully to do the same thing with the same horse. But I'm a lighter rider and I've been giving Sky an athlete's nutrition—the highest quality grain to be found—preparing for this."

When Ryan rubbed his hands together, Sam remembered last week, when she'd been alone on Gold Dust Ranch.

Right after Jen's accident, Ross had driven Jen to the hospital and Lila had gone to meet them after making Sam promise to stay at Gold Dust, to tell Jed, Jen's father, what had happened. After caring for Silly, Sam had wandered over to the barn and heard the rush of grain from a scoop and seen Ryan with Sky Ranger, the Thoroughbred gelding who was sleek and fast as a greyhound.

Hotspot came from running stock, too, so it would be a fair race, but Ryan hadn't said he was stalking the Appaloosa mare. He'd said "stalking the herd," like his father had.

Sam recalled one rainy morning on her first cattle drive. From her sleeping bag she'd heard hooves splattering mud and looked up to see Linc ride out on Sky Ranger, determined to chase down the Phantom.

Now, when Sam looked at Ryan's photos of the maps on his bedroom wall, she felt sick.

Ryan was entitled to go after Hotspot, but . . .

"Do the pins in those maps show where she's been spotted?" Sam asked.

"That's almost right," Ryan encouraged her.

"The Phantom's herd?" Sam's voice turned shrill as she demanded, "You've been tracking the Phantom's herd?"

The screen door opened. Lila handed Ryan an empty glass for lemonade, then asked, "Everything all right out here?"

"Yeah, Mom," Jen said. "Sam's just—" Jen must have felt the accusation from Sam's eyes, because she broke off. "We're fine."

Waiting for Jen's mom to leave, Sam gripped her hands into fists so tight, she felt her fingernails press into her palms. Finally the screen door closed again.

"I'm not fine," Sam said quietly.

"All right, then. Yes, I've talked with people who've spotted that wild band, the band Hotspot's traveling with." Ryan let his words sink in, then asked, "Sam, what's the difference? I've gotten information from several sources. I'm putting it together. So what?"

Wasn't it bad enough that Pam and her mother would see the Phantom? Now Ryan would be after him, too. He'd see the Phantom and fall under his spell.

Sam knew she wasn't being selfish. If she didn't shield the stallion from other people, someone was bound to turn greedy.

Sam swallowed. "I can't explain."

"Would you rather have me just blundering across the range on my own?"

"Of course not," Sam said. "I don't want you to get lost, but—"

Sam knew it would be rude to say what she was thinking. Ryan's father was obsessed with the stallion. If Ryan knew where to find the Phantom, he'd probably tell Linc.

"But what?" Ryan asked.

"Who are your sources?" Sam demanded.

Ryan arranged the maps. As he talked, he pointed out meadows and springs mentioned to him by Caleb Sawyer, the hermit of Snake's Head Peak. He indicated trails and canyons both Jen and Mrs. Coley had told him about.

"These are gullies, a *playa*, water holes, and washes my father admitted got the best of him when he was after the stallion," Ryan said, ignoring the fact that Linc's actions were illegal.

Next, Ryan's index finger tapped places he'd heard about from Mrs. Allen, Sheriff Ballard, Brynna, and Karl Mannix, the horse thief.

"My information indicates the herd has six favorite habitats." Tilting his head to one side, as if he were joking, Ryan added, "Those details came from almost everyone in the county, except you and Jake Ely."

Sam felt dizzy, and it wasn't from the heat.

Ryan fidgeted in his chair. He watched Jen, obviously waiting for congratulations.

"These sightings of the Phantom go back over three years," he boasted.

He knew, and so did Sam, that Jen admired his calculated, analytical approach to tracking the herd, but she sat silent.

When she cupped her hand over her bandages, Sam knew why.

"Jen, does your rib hurt?"

Lips pressed together, Jen shook her head.

As if he thought Sam's question were meant to distract him, Ryan protested, "I assure both of you that I only want Hotspot."

Jen met Sam's eyes. They both heard the plea in his words.

"I believe you," Sam said, but she couldn't help thinking of Golden Rose, the palomino mare Ryan had kept hidden in the ghost town of Nugget. He'd known she belonged to someone else. Still, he'd kept her.

Images of Nugget led to thoughts of prospectors who'd sworn they'd be level-headed amid a stampede for riches. But once they'd begun digging the dirt and panning the water of nearby streams, once they'd seen the glitter of precious minerals, the miners had given in to obsessions for gold nuggets and veins of silver.

Ryan wouldn't know he wanted the silver stallion until he saw him.

"So then you'll help me?" Ryan asked.

Sam looked to Jen for advice, but her friend had reached for the stack of schoolbooks. Wincing, Jen stretched until her hand clamped on a brand new calculus book. Then she settled it on her lap with a sigh of satisfaction.

Poor Jen, Sam thought. She must feel left out. First, her parents had kept her from going back to school. Now her rib kept her from joining Ryan's search for Hotspot. Something told Sam that Jen wouldn't enjoy hearing that Sam's old best friend was coming to town.

Lila opened the screen door. "Sam?" she said, but her eyes studied Jen, and Sam knew Lila had given up on her daughter's good judgment. "It's time I called your Gram, don't you think?"

Before Sam could agree, Ryan spoke up.

"Don't bother, Mrs. Kenworthy. I'll take Samantha home. We have things to discuss."

"Fine," Lila said, but Sam wasn't so sure.

"Jen, is that okay?" Sam asked. No way would she ride with Ryan, alone, if it made her best friend jealous. "Jen?"

One of Jen's braids had worked loose from its hairpins. It exposed the sunburned part on her scalp and hung down like the ear of a sad puppy.

Jen didn't fix it. She'd didn't answer. She didn't even look up from the math book.

Ryan shook his head impatiently, stood, and started walking toward the circular driveway where his family's cars were parked.

"Jen," Sam repeated once Ryan was too far away to hear her, "do you want me to wait? Or is it okay if I go with Ryan and save Gram a drive over here? I don't mind waiting. Really."

Jen was probably just engrossed in the wonders of calculus, but Sam had to make sure.

"I know I'm less fascinating than math, but give me a sign that you hear me, okay?" Sam snatched up her friend's hand. "Squeeze once for *yes* and twice for *no*."

Finally Jen looked up. She gave a weak smile. "Sure, go ahead. Help him find his horse. Anything that will help him stand up to his dad is fine with me. Besides, I know you don't like him like I do."

The sun glinted on the lenses of Jen's glasses, hiding her eyes so that Sam couldn't tell what Jen meant by that last bit.

"I'll call you tonight," Sam promised.

"Will you?" Jen asked.

"Sure," Sam said. Then she gave her friend's hand a single squeeze and left.

Chapter Four ↣

A horse galloped far off in the distance, where the bone-white *playa* met blue Nevada sky.

Sam spotted it after she and Ryan had left Gold Dust Ranch, turned left, and started driving toward River Bend Ranch. She'd been staring in the direction of Lost Canyon, wondering if Pam and her mother had arrived yet.

It probably wasn't a mustang. Not in the late afternoon. Not in this heat. Not out in the open. Mustangs craved shade and coolness just like other animals.

Did the horse have a rider she couldn't make out through the dust and distance? Was it really even there? She could be so fixated on the Phantom that she was seeing things. It wouldn't be the first time.

Sam pulled her eyes away from the fleet figure. Then she turned sideways, shoulder to the windshield, as Ryan repeated a question he was asking for the second time.

". . . aren't on my map?"

"I'm sorry," Sam apologized, shaking her head as if she could dislodge the image of the running horse. "What did you say?"

"I asked if there are places, besides the six I've listed, where you've sighted the Phantom?"

"Sure," Sam answered.

"If I promise not to lay a finger on the stallion, will you tell me about them?"

"No, Ryan. I haven't told anyone."

Ryan looked skeptical.

"I haven't and I won't," she insisted. "But you did a really nice job on that map, from what I can tell in the photographs."

"I'm flattered," Ryan said, his fingers tightening on the steering wheel. He slanted his head left, grimaced as if the sun glare on the windshield was aimed only at him, then snatched up sunglasses from the car's console. He stabbed them over his ears so forcefully, Sam winced.

Ryan was awfully worked up about her refusal to answer his questions, so she tried to lead the conversation in a different direction. "What are you going to study in college?"

"Nothing," he snapped. "I want to take over the ranch once my father loses interest in it."

No, Sam thought. The Kenworthys longed to buy their ranch back someday. She still hoped a miracle would make it happen.

"And he *will* lose interest," Ryan continued, "make no mistake about that."

Sam held her breath as her mind raced. The Kenworthys needed the ranch to continue their palomino breeding program, Fire and Ice. She and Jen daydreamed about growing up to run River Bend and Gold Dust, living next door to each other.

Trust a Slocum to mess everything up. Unless . . .

Sam shot Ryan a calculating look. Maybe there was another way. Not as good, but if Jen and Ryan officially became boyfriend and girlfriend, she supposed they might get married. Jen would have her ranch back.

What would be even better, since she didn't really trust Ryan, was if they got engaged, then Ryan fell in love with someone else. Then, out of guilt he might just give Jen the ranch. Sam smiled at her tangled fantasy. Of course it was far-fetched, but it could happen.

As if he'd noticed her mind drifting, Ryan added, "Learning the ways of the West are college enough for me right now."

Sam knew it wouldn't do any good to tell Ryan that most successful ranchers had attended college.

Many continued their education through classes on the Internet or agricultural extension programs, too. If his daydream came true, he'd find out for himself.

And there was another reason Sam didn't argue with him.

The dark horse's silhouette was clearer now. Its size, strong gait, and fluttering tail—probably black—looked familiar.

"Are you telling me Jake Ely doesn't know where to find that mustang stallion?" Ryan blurted. "Your Phantom?"

"I'm not saying he doesn't know. I'm afraid he might," Sam admitted. "But if he knows, I sure didn't tell him. And if he knows, I doubt he'd tell you or anyone else."

Jake didn't love the Phantom like she did, but he respected the horse as he did all wild things. Besides, she and Jake were friends. He knew revealing the stallion's hidden valley would end that friendship.

"I only want Hotspot." Ryan pronounced each syllable in the sentence. It was annoying and Sam was already running out of patience when he added, "Why can't you just take me at my word?"

"Gee, I don't know, Ryan. Maybe it's because the last time I did, I ended up in a police car?"

Ryan drove in silence and Sam told herself she shouldn't feel a bit bad for reminding him that he was to blame for hiding Hotspot and Shy Boots near Cowkiller Caldera. It was his fault Hotspot was running with the mustangs and pure luck Shy Boots hadn't died without her.

Sam sighed. If she punished Ryan by making him do this on his own, she'd be punishing Shy Boots, too.

Besides, she was pretty sure Hotspot would be happier at Gold Dust Ranch. The last time Sam had seen her, the mare had still worn her leather halter and she'd been trying to decide whether to graze alongside the Phantom's wild mares or the captive mustangs in Mrs. Allen's pasture.

Sam felt her stubbornness melting. "I'll help you get started," Sam agreed, but she cut Ryan's thanks short when she realized the dark horse on the horizon was Witch. "That's Jake's horse."

"Why would he be running alongside it instead of riding?" Ryan asked, and Sam saw he was right.

Jake's sweat-shiny arms swung in a relaxed rhythm. His long strides kept him running in the shadow of the black Quarter Horse mare.

"He's in training for the cross-country team," Sam said as she noticed Jake's green-and-gold Darton High shorts and T-shirt with hacked-off sleeves.

"So we shouldn't stop and offer him a ride?" Ryan asked.

"No, he hates to be interrupted," Sam said as she lowered the car window. "We'll just wave as we go past."

"If you say so," Ryan answered.

Hot sage and sand scented the desert air that

invaded the car. As Sam leaned from the open window, she wondered what caused the surge of satisfaction at the heat hitting her face.

Jake ran at the roadside, just ahead. She heard his shoes pounding pavement and his steady breaths.

Witch snorted, but she didn't shy when Ryan slowed down. The mare kept pace with Jake, as if they were yoked in a team.

Jake's head turned slowly as the Mercedes drew alongside. His black hair swept back from flushed cheekbones and a set jaw. He nodded in response to Sam's wave, but he looked hypnotized, focused on each stride, each footfall, adding up the miles.

As they pulled past, Ryan looked into his rearview mirror.

"You do realize that mare is not on a lead line. She's running at heel, like a dog."

Witch would stay there, too. Even if a jackrabbit sped across her path or a low-flying hawk dropped to snatch up dinner, the mare wouldn't bolt away from her master.

"Jake's really good with horses," Sam said.

"I daresay he is," Ryan responded.

"Besides, she loves him," Sam said. When Ryan stayed silent, she glanced over at him. Was it just her imagination that he looked envious?

They'd almost reached the La Charla River when Ryan said, "It's not about the money."

"What are you talking about?" Sam asked.

"Catching Hotspot. I want what's best for Shy Boots."

"I know. But Ryan, all you've got is a list of places. You need—" Sam broke off. It hadn't been luck that she'd seen the Phantom so many times. "—some kind of instinct."

"I've got something better," Ryan insisted. "A plan. Once I've found her, I'll chase her down, just like Jake did with that pinto."

Chase her down. Put that way, Jake's capture of Star Shower sounded cruel, but it hadn't been. Running together day and night, Jake and the filly had formed a herd bond before they'd ever touched.

"Jake had his grandfather to show him how to do that," Sam pointed out.

"*My* grandfathers aren't shamen. One is an investment banker in Boston and the other owns Leeds of London department store." Ryan squared his shoulders. "I can do this on my own."

"You'll still need a relay of horses," Sam told him.

"I thought of that," Ryan said, nodding. "I'll ask Mrs. Allen's permission to use Roman along with Sky."

"They'd be good," Sam said, but she shifted in her seat.

Roman was the liver chestnut mustang Ryan had ridden in the Superbowl of Horsemanship. The gelding had stamina and he'd responded well to Ryan's skills, but Sam hadn't felt the same about Roman since he'd fought with the Phantom when the stallion had been temporarily deaf.

She knew what she'd seen had been a natural battle for dominance, but it was hard to erase the mental picture of Roman's rearing challenge. His long mane and the untrimmed hair under his cheeks and chin had made Roman look primitive and fierce.

"Don't forget to tell Brynna what you're doing," Sam cautioned as the Mercedes rolled over the bridge, headed for River Bend's ranch yard. "Otherwise, you'll be cited for harassing the wild horses."

"Of course," Ryan promised, then he braked to a sudden stop. "Here now, what's this?"

Blaze, the ranch Border collie, stood with head lowered and hackles raised, blocking the path of the Mercedes.

Ryan gave the car's horn a tap, but Blaze met the sound with a volley of low barks and refused to move.

"I guess he doesn't recognize the car," Sam said, as she rolled down the window to call to the dog. "Hey Blaze, it's okay. It's me."

With a grumbling growl, Blaze moved aside. Sam thought he glared back over his shoulder as if she were a traitor.

"Crazy dog," she said.

"Not really," Ryan said. "You're just as suspicious."

"Just think about helping me," Ryan said. "I promise I won't become smitten with your stallion.

Let me repeat, I'm only interested in bringing Hotspot home."

Feelings in a tangle, Sam said, "Yeah, well, first you have to find her."

"I promise you wouldn't be sorry," Ryan told her.

But Sam wasn't so sure.

Chapter Five ❧

Sam was still shaking her head at Ryan's stubbornness as she crossed the ranch yard toward Brynna.

Her stepmother wore her khaki uniform and a frizzled French braid, so she must have just arrived home, but she hadn't hurried into the cool house. She stood at the pasture fence, leaning as far forward as her pregnancy would allow, kissing her mare's copper-colored nose.

Flushed and freckled, Brynna smiled as Sam approached.

"Hi, how was school?" Brynna called.

Sam had only begun to tell Brynna about her classes when Ace approached the fence and stopped just out of reach.

"Ace," Sam called. She made a smooching sound and he walked a step closer.

"He's going to make you beg," Brynna said.

Brynna's horse, Penny, flattened her ears, telling Ace to keep his distance, but the bay mustang continued to advance.

"I'm sorry there's not time for a ride, but tomorrow for sure," Sam told her horse. He nuzzled her empty palm as she rubbed his neck.

"Tomorrow?" Brynna asked.

"Pam will be here," Sam said. "I'm going out to Lost Canyon to see her."

"Great," Brynna said. She didn't sound all that enthusiastic, but she didn't know Pam. Or maybe she was just enthralled with watching her blind mare nibble her sleeve. "How's Jen doing?"

"Fine, but she's kind of tired." Sam frowned and worked her fingers through a tangle in Ace's black mane. "And she's worried. Her dad still doesn't want her to go back to school even when she's recovered."

Sam was about to tell Brynna about Shy Boots, too, and how Jen would have to take care of him, when her stepmother asked an unexpected question.

"How's Jen feel about Pam showing up?"

Sam's hands went still in Ace's mane. There was something almost sly in Brynna's tone, but her eyebrows were lifted in real concern.

"I didn't get a chance to tell her, but what do you mean, how does she feel?" Sam shook her head in pretend confusion. She wanted to believe worrying over Jen's jealousy was childish.

Brynna shrugged. "You know, since Pam was your best friend in San Francisco."

"They're both my friends," Sam said, and though she knew it was unfair, she felt annoyed at Brynna for making her face this possibility. "Why wouldn't that be okay with Jen?"

Brynna looked away for a second, and when she looked back, Sam got the feeling her stepmother wished she hadn't brought the whole subject up.

"Sometimes, three isn't a great number for friends," Brynna pointed out. "You know, two's company and three's a crowd?"

"I don't know what you're talking about," Sam snapped. Even to herself, she sounded bratty, but what if Brynna was right?

Reacting to her harsh tone, Ace backed away from Sam's hands.

"Don't bite my head off, Sam," Brynna began, but then Penny snorted.

The mare's sightless eyes rolled in wariness, and that's probably what made Brynna angry.

"And you can take your hands off your hips, young lady."

Sam did.

"I only mentioned an issue you might want to be sensitive to," Brynna said quietly. "Especially since Jen is bound to be feeling a little confined."

Jen *was* feeling confined and bored, but Sam tried to hope for the best.

"Jen's not the jealous type," Sam insisted, although she knew Jen had a jealous streak a mile wide when it came to Jake. And Callie. But maybe that was just part of the loyalty that made Jen such a good friend. "Besides, they're not even going to be around each other."

"Okay," Brynna said.

"If you want to worry about one of my friends . . ." Sam began.

"I don't—"

"Worry about Jake," Sam said. She watched Ace cross the pasture. Even her horse was fed up with her. "He's hardly spoken to me since he cut his hair and went off on his college tour—"

"He's only been back a few days."

"—and now all he's doing is training for cross country. In fact, I'm going in to call him," Sam said.

She turned toward the house. Jake's steady pace should have taken him to Three Ponies Ranch by now. If she hurried, she could catch him before he ducked into the shower, had dinner, or started homework.

Blaze fell into step with Sam, giving his tail a low wag to ask if he was forgiven for blocking the bridge with his body.

"You're a good boy, Blaze," she said, rumpling his silky ears. "You can't be too careful." She lowered her voice to a whisper. "In fact, I think I'll ask Jake what he thinks of Ryan's plan."

"Nice talking to you, too, honey," Brynna called after her.

Realizing she'd just walked off without a good-bye, Sam listened for resentment in her stepmother's voice, but she didn't hear it. In fact, Brynna sounded almost amused.

Since amusement was the last thing Sam felt over Jake, she kept walking toward the kitchen.

Gram's knife sliced through long onions that smelled fresh and green.

"I'm making a salad that even your father will love," Gram said, glancing toward chicken strips sputtering with grated ginger in a skillet.

"Yum," Sam said.

"You're a little late," Gram added. "Everything okay over at the Kenworthys?"

"Sure," Sam said. Then, because there was no privacy in the house and if you wanted to use the phone you had to stand in the kitchen, Sam added, "Ryan's colt is kind of sickly, so he's going to go out and try to catch Hotspot."

Gram made a disapproving hum as she scraped the onions from her cutting board into the skillet.

"Hope he checked that out with Brynna." Gram raised her voice over the renewed sputtering.

"He said he would," Sam said, edging toward the phone.

"Slocums and wild horses are bad business," Gram added.

"Tell me about it," Sam said, but when Gram looked up, alarmed, Sam added, "I think Ryan's okay."

Poking the chicken and onions with a wooden spoon, Gram said, "One can only hope."

"I'm going to call Jake," Sam said.

Gram nodded, but she was more focused on measuring soy sauce than on Sam's dialing.

Jake's dad answered the phone at Three Ponies Ranch and Sam was glad. He wouldn't ask her about her classes or Jen. You never had to worry about unnecessary conversation with Luke Ely. If anything, he was quieter than his sons.

"Hello," said Luke Ely.

"Hi," Sam began.

"Jake?" Luke hollered. Then, as an explanation, he added, "Sam."

She heard the phone change hands.

"Hey," Jake said.

"How was your run?" Sam asked. "Pretty good?"

"Yeah."

"Do you think you're as competitive as you were last year?"

"Yeah," Jake said.

Jake was one of the best runners in the state. If he had another winning season, he'd have his choice of scholarships to good colleges. She'd learned that information from the local newspaper, which was a good thing, because she never would have heard it from Jake.

Now she was remembering that the only thing more frustrating than talking to Jake in person was trying to talk to him on the phone.

"Ryan's going to try to catch Hotspot," Sam began.

"Yeah?" Jake asked.

"Out of the Phantom's herd," Sam emphasized. "If she's still with him. Do you know if she is?"

"Naw," Jake said.

"So, what do you think?" Sam asked.

"Don't know if I should shower first or eat. Food makes me sick when I first get in."

Sam lowered the phone from her ear and glared at it. Was Jake listening to what she'd been saying?

"Jake!" Sam would have started all over again if she hadn't heard him snort with enjoyment at her irritation. "Look, can he do it without messing things up with the herd? Should I help him?"

"You want to?" Jake asked.

"What do you mean, do I want to?" Sam sputtered.

Jake stayed quiet, giving her no hint whether he meant did she want to hang around with Ryan, did she want to snatch Hotspot away from the Phantom, or any of a dozen other possibilities.

"There's that thing they say—hey, give it!" Jake

broke off and Sam heard scuffling, male shouts about the last sports drink in the refrigerator, and finally she heard Jake gulping liquid like a thirsty horse.

As she waited for him to finish, Sam realized her eyes were closed and she was gripping her forehead with one hand.

"What thing?" she asked, at last.

"Huh?"

"What thing do they say?" Sam repeated.

"I don't know, it's something like 'keep your friends close, but your enemies closer,'" Jake told her.

"I don't understand."

More wrestling sounds hid Jake's response. Or maybe there wasn't one.

When she heard a hammering sound, Sam realized he'd dropped the phone. Then she heard Mrs. Ely calling everyone to the dinner table.

Since it wasn't very likely Jake had anything else to say, Sam hung up.

Sam loved Gram's chicken salad and her English homework was easy, but she decided it wasn't her day for good phone calls.

She hadn't heard from Pam, so Sam guessed she'd just have to ride over to Lost Canyon tomorrow. Maybe she'd go with Ryan, because she'd finally figured out what Jake's puzzling comment had meant.

Keep your friends close and your enemies closer, Jake had said. If she rode with Ryan, she could keep an eye on him and make sure he didn't locate the Phantom and decide he had to have him.

It was weird calling Ryan, but the instant she finished washing the dishes, Sam did it.

"So you've considered the merits of my plan and you've decided to tell me where the Great One hides, right?" Ryan asked.

He sounded entirely too smug, but Sam reminded herself she was doing this for the horses.

"Not exactly," Sam said. "I'll ride with you when I can, though, and help you narrow your search."

And she would. Ryan's map showed War Drum Flats, Lost Canyon, the area around Blind Faith Mustang Sanctuary, Snake's Head Peak, Fishbait Springs, and Cowkiller Caldera. He already knew mustangs haunted those areas, but she could show him within yards, not miles, where the herd had been.

Sam was congratulating herself on her own maturity when Ryan cut her off.

"Thanks for the lovely offer," he began, and Sam could hear Ryan's "however," though he hadn't said it.

After all his begging was he going to turn her down?

"All I'm requesting is how do I put this? An 'X marks the spot.'" Ryan gave a low chuckle. "You know—like they have on treasure maps?"

For a second, Sam wondered if Gram had left the oven on full blast, because it didn't seem possible her face could turn this hot from anger.

"Simply tell me the best place to look for the Phantom's herd," Ryan clarified. "I'll be riding alone."

She couldn't fight with Ryan right here and now, with Gram standing a few feet away, but she had to say something.

"So, you just want sort of a cheat sheet from me?" Sam thought she did a good job of asking the question pleasantly.

"I'm not sure what that is," Ryan said, "but I'm certainly not requesting something unsavory."

Yeah, you are, Sam thought.

"After all, we're friends," he added.

Ryan wasn't trying to buy a shortcut with money, like his father did, but couldn't he hear himself trying to buy it with friendship?

Sam knew she wouldn't have pointed that out, even if she hadn't suddenly remembered Jen. She should have called Jen hours ago.

"Actually, I was calling to tell you I think you're on the right track with the places you're looking and to offer to let Brynna know your plan, to save you a phone call."

You wimp, Sam told herself, but after Ryan accepted her offer and she hung up the phone, Sam decided she'd been nice to him for Jen.

She would have told Jen that, but her best friend called first, sounding gloomy and critical.

"Thanks for calling like you promised," Jen said right away.

"It's not like I forgot," Sam protested. "I was waiting until I finished my homework, sort of like looking forward to dessert," Sam teased.

Jen didn't laugh. She zoomed straight to what she wanted to know.

"So, did you and Ryan have fun?"

"Not really," Sam answered.

"Did you plan how to catch Hotspot?" Jen asked.

"No more than we did at your house," Sam said. "I won't take him to any secret places and he's already got the others on his map."

What could she say to make Jen laugh? Sam's mind raced. She considered telling Jen about her daydream, that Jen would marry Ryan and get Gold Dust Ranch back, but Jen didn't sound like she was in the mood for far-fetched fantasy.

"What aren't you telling me?" Jen demanded.

"Nothing," Sam said and then, because that wasn't exactly true and Jen had already picked up on her hesitation, Sam amended, "Something stupid."

"About Ryan?"

"Well, sort of," Sam said. Then, just when she was about to change the subject and tell Jen about Pam, she hesitated again. Of course Jen heard something in her delay that made her think something major was going on.

"Look, Sam, he's trying to be a good guy."

"I know—"

"Just give him a chance, okay?"

Jen wasn't being fair, but she was probably miserable. Sam wouldn't trade places with her for anything. She tried really hard to be understanding.

"I wasn't going to say anything bad, Jen," she told her friend, but Jen didn't seem to hear.

"Think of that first day we met him," Jen said. "Remember? When the cougar was eating his dad's buffet? Ryan was so cute. He wouldn't let anyone hurt the cat. And don't forget he tamed Roman. Anyone else looking at that horse would only see its bad conformation—"

"Jen—"

"Plus, he didn't abandon me after Sky went psycho in that race. . . ."

Sam blinked. How could Jen think that counted in Ryan's favor? It was what any friend—no, what any *decent human*—would do!

"And when I was in the hospital, he brought me roses."

Sam stared at the kitchen ceiling and counted to ten. By the time she finished, it sounded as if Jen had finally run down.

"I know he did. He was great while you were in the hospital," Sam said. "He's not a bad guy, and I think he's really . . . grown up while he's been here."

Sam thought she'd chosen her words well, because Jen was quiet, as if she didn't hear anything to contradict.

"Sorry I went off on you," Jen said, finally. "It's not like you're going to steal my boyfriend. In the first place, you've made it quite apparent that Ryan's not your type."

"I have a type?" Sam blurted and for some reason, the question sent Jen into a gale of giggles and Sam couldn't help but join in.

"Ow, ow, ow," Jen said finally. "Don't do that. It kills my ribs."

Even though Sam had no idea what had made her friend laugh, it was wonderful to hear her do it. And she couldn't bring up Pam now, just in case her paranoia over Jen's jealousy came true.

Tomorrow would be soon enough.

Chapter Six ❧

Galloping hooves hammered in Sam's dream. She woke slowly, opening her eyes to her own dark bedroom where the sound of hooves made no sense.

I was dreaming, she thought.

Falling asleep had been hard because she couldn't stop picturing Hotspot, Shy Boots, the Phantom, Roman, and—what was that sound?

Sam rolled on her side and faced her bedroom window. White curtains stirred in a cool breeze. She pulled up a blanket she'd tossed away in the night. The coziness should have made her sleepy, but it didn't.

She sat up on the edge of her bed, wide awake. She stared so hard she felt her eyelashes touch the skin beneath her eyebrows. She listened so intently, she thought she could hear blood whooshing through her own veins.

There. Four hoofbeats, four more, and four more. They struck so close together, they could have come from several horses, not just one.

With one long step, Sam made it to her window in time to see a single horse running along the far bank of the La Charla River.

Was it a paint? Before she knew, the horse vanished upstream. But there'd been a flash of white. Not silver, so it wasn't her stallion. Still, something told Sam to go take a look.

It had run with the smooth, collected gait of a trained horse, but she hadn't recognized it. Even half awake and blinking the sleep from her eyes, Sam knew it wasn't Jake's Shooting Star or one of Mrs. Allen's old mares. Sweetheart was River Bend's only paint, and she lived in town now, being ridden by children as a therapy horse.

Maybe the horse was running with the Phantom's band, Sam thought as she tiptoed down the stairs. Maybe the whole herd was out there and she could just smooch to Hotspot and deliver her to Ryan. But she had to hurry.

Sam didn't change out of the huge T-shirt she'd worn to bed as a nightgown, but she pulled jeans on under it and slipped her feet into a pair of sandals.

She tiptoed down the stairs, hoping the sandals wouldn't slap her heels.

Dad might have heard her anyway. He was an awfully light sleeper, but she didn't hear the bedsprings shift or the floor overhead creak.

Her mind kept replaying those hoofbeats. They'd sounded too close to the ranch to have come from a mustang. The Phantom might wade into the middle of the La Charla, himself, but he didn't allow his herd to cross from the wild side of the river to the banks on the River Bend side.

Sam was almost down the stairs when the grandfather clock's chimes made her gasp and nearly trip. *Keep going*, she told herself.

Four o'clock. It was so late, it was early. She might not have time to go back to sleep after she checked out this horse. Could she make it through a school day on two hours' less sleep than usual?

She'd have to do it. For a chance to see the Phantom, she'd skip sleep for ten nights!

Cougar was nowhere around, but Blaze whined when Sam shut him inside the house. She felt sorry for him, but she didn't take time to apologize. She'd already wasted too much time getting outside.

A hen fluttered in the chicken coop as Sam passed it. A coyote yapped from the ridge as she crossed the ranch yard and noticed the dark shapes of horses watching her from the pasture.

The galloping horse was probably gone by now. She'd spent five stupid minutes getting this far. She should have rushed faster.

Sam had already reached the center of the bridge when she saw she was wrong.

The horse was still there, and it wasn't alone.

The charcoal-gray sky showed a pale orange smear just over the mountains. By the faint light, Sam made out a running horse with white smudges. It was no paint, she realized. It was an Appaloosa. Hotspot.

The young mare galloped with head high, drinking in the scent of dewy sagebrush and dawn. Born to run, she dashed effortlessly along the river, about a half mile in one direction, before wheeling to run back the other way.

Sam searched for the Phantom, but didn't see him.

Still, Hotspot wasn't alone.

Three, no, four horses moved in silhouette beyond the young mare.

They'd come here with Hotspot, but they stood apart from her. They were like fingers and a thumb, she decided. Connected, but while the other four horses pressed together, Hotspot split off alone.

That was how Hotspot had acted when the wild herd had lived at Blind Faith Mustang Sanctuary, after the fire. With the Phantom injured and distracted, the wild herd had scattered into small family groups, but Hotspot had hovered between the wild mustangs and those who lived in the sanctuary. Now, she was still unsure of her place.

And the other horses were clearly unsure of her,

too. After all, what did she add to the herd? She had speed, but not sense. She knew how to step primly past irrigation sprinklers or accidentally dropped curry combs, but would she recognize the scent of saddle leather or the crunch of tires on sand as threats?

Probably not, Sam thought, and right then, Hotspot caught sight of her and slid to a stop.

The Appaloosa directed her full attention at Sam. Chocolate ears and nose pointed straight at her. Hotspot swished her tail and began dancing restlessly in place, but her gaze never wavered.

Sam imagined the mare was deciding whether she should stay on the fringes of the herd, or cross over the river and return to civilization and her foal.

If Hotspot was curious and uncertain about Sam, the wild horses weren't. They knew exactly what she represented.

Danger.

Even though they treated Hotspot as an outsider, the other horses swept her into the safety of the herd. But as the others fled toward the mountains, Hotspot veered off again.

The biggest of the four other horses broke away after her. It was hard to tell in the half light, but Sam was pretty sure it was the honey-brown mare, the Phantom's lead mare, that darted after Hotspot, quick as Ace after a naughty calf.

Hotspot refused to go along. She pretended to

obey when the mare flattened her ears, but then she dawdled, making the lead mare backtrack to round her up. When the big mare bumped shoulders with Hotspot, the Appaloosa gave a halfhearted rear.

She just doesn't know the order of things, Sam was thinking, when she suddenly caught a sound and movement from the corner of her eye. Like a white thundercloud rumbling down from a nook between the foothills, the Phantom descended on the other horses.

One glimpse of the impatient stallion was enough to make the four mares forget about Hotspot. Heads level, tails streaming, three set off instantly to rejoin the rest of the hidden herd. Even the lead mare was willing to leave Hotspot to her punishment.

Trotting and shaking her head, the lead mare seemed to have decided Hotspot deserved what was coming to her.

"What are you thinking?" Sam whispered toward the Appaloosa.

Giddy instead of chastened at the sight of the stallion, Hotspot cantered to meet him.

Head held high, even when he lowered his in a snaking, herding motion, Hotspot greeted him as her buddy instead of her king.

How could she have learned so little in two months?

The Phantom wasn't going to make allowances for her ignorance, either. Even though he knew Sam presented no threat, she was a human. Hotspot should have fled as she'd been told.

Cavorting out of his path, Hotspot pranced and tossed her mane, showing the stallion he was missing all the fun. Only when his head struck out, open-mouthed, and dealt her a hard bite on the rump did Hotspot give an offended squeal of understanding.

With a last glance toward Sam and River Bend Ranch, she wheeled away.

Legs flying in smooth strides, she moved up the hillside like a dark bird. She caught the other mares without even trying, then kept running until she was out of sight.

The Phantom didn't look after the wayward mare. Instead he gazed toward the bridge, toward Sam.

She held her breath.

Come to me, Zanzibar, she thought, aiming every bit of longing toward him. *C'mon boy, please.*

When was the last time she'd seen the stallion? The last time she'd touched him? She didn't know. The silver stallion, with his drifting mane and steady stare, held her hypnotized. Sam watched with lips parted. She took shallow, silent breaths, so that even that faint sound wouldn't disturb him.

Pale and furious, he rose into a full rear. Soundlessly, his forelegs pawed the air. When he lowered to all fours, he shook his head, scolding Sam too, as if she were responsible for the Appaloosa's defiance.

"Not me," Sam whispered to the stallion. "If it

were my choice, she'd be safe at home with her baby, not out on the range, making trouble for you."

With a snort, the stallion settled back on his haunches, then swiveled away from her and the ranch where he'd once lived. He departed at a regal trot, leaving Sam alone in the hazy morning light.

War Drum Flats fit like a shallow bowl into the surrounding land. Sparse sage and scattered gray rocks surrounded a small desert lake. It wasn't a lush place to graze, but it was a safe place for a herd to drink its fill, then stand and enjoy cool, watery motion on run-tested legs.

No brush grew tall enough to hide humans, coyotes, or other predators bent on snatching colts, and after seeing the Phantom that morning, Sam didn't really expect to see him again in the afternoon.

Still, she watched the stairstep mesas to the east. They were shaped like stone benches, perfect perches for a sentry stallion watching others drink down below.

Nothing could approach the lake at War Drum Flats in secret.

As Sam rode Ace toward the lake, she yawned, then forced herself to be alert. She knew wild eyes watched her, but she saw no horses, only a flutter of wings as birds rose from the lake's surface to drift away like dozens of paper airplanes.

She wasn't out here to find wild horses, or Ryan.

She was looking for Pam and her mother.

"An old green truck with a brown camper, but we'll have a full base camp set up. You won't be able to miss us," Pam had said.

Sam glanced at the watch on her right wrist.

It wasn't quite four o'clock on this day that felt like it would never end.

Her predawn encounter with the wild horses had been wonderful, and she'd earned praise from the whole family for starting coffee and breakfast before anyone else was awake.

Standing at the bus stop later, she'd seen Ryan riding out on Sky Ranger. The Thoroughbred's perfectly groomed hide had looked oiled and Ryan had posted to the gelding's trot from an English saddle. Horse and rider looked determined to get the job of finding Hotspot done in a single day.

She could have called out to him and told him what she'd seen, but she knew it wouldn't have helped. In two hours, the horses could have gone anywhere.

Besides, Ryan wouldn't welcome her interference. He only wanted to know the location of the Phantom's secret valley.

Now, Sam shrugged as she rode along. Ryan was determined to show Linc that he could catch his mare on his own. If she'd read Hotspot right, the Appaloosa would be willing to be caught.

Despite her early wakening, Sam's classes had

gone fine and after school, she'd been pleased that Mrs. Coley, Gold Dust Ranch's housekeeper, had suggested Sam ride home with her and Rachel, Ryan's twin, since Sam was taking Jen's homework to Gold Dust Ranch anyway.

Sharing the backseat with a silent Rachel made the trip interminable, but she couldn't help comparing the twins.

Both had sleek coffee-brown hair, but Ryan didn't try to hide the intelligence in his dark eyes. Rachel's eyes, rimmed with black eyeliner, rarely landed on anything long enough for Sam to read their expression.

During the ride home, she'd ignored Sam, passing the time talking on her cell phone until she lost service. She'd dropped the phone on the seat beside her and dug a second, tinier phone from her purse. When that one failed to connect as well, she'd thrown it on the floor near Sam's feet.

"One more year in this primitive, vulgar place may be more than I can stand," Rachel had snarled.

"Brynna's always losing cell service," Sam had sympathized. "She thinks the truck radios are more dependable than her government phone."

Rachel hadn't said a word in return. She'd given Sam a blank, slightly resentful look. The comment was of no interest, Rachel's eyes said, and she begrudged the consumption of air used to make it.

But then, when Sam took out her literature book and began reading her homework assignment, Rachel had crossed her arms and looked insulted.

When they'd reached Gold Dust Ranch, Rachel had flounced from the car, leaving Sam to thank Mrs. Coley.

"You're welcome, Sam," Mrs. Coley had said with such appreciation that Sam guessed Rachel—even when she wasn't miffed—didn't show much gratitude. "I talked with your Gram earlier today at a planning meeting for the church harvest dinner, and she said to tell you she'd be along to pick you up—" Mrs. Coley glanced at her watch. "—about now. So, you'd better scurry over to the Kenworthys' place and get your visiting done fast."

Sam had lingered by the car for a minute, searching the pastures for a sign of Hotspot, but Shy Boots and Princess Kitty grazed alone in their paddock, and Sam was pretty sure that's where Ryan would have put the Appaloosa mare if he'd found her.

Still, Sam had to ask.

"Ryan hasn't come back with Hotspot, has he?" she asked Mrs. Coley.

"I haven't seen him since early this morning. He left before breakfast—just grabbed some granola and an apple, then headed out the door. Linc had plenty to say about Ryan 'wasting his time' instead of letting BLM bring her in, so Ryan's fighting an uphill battle, but I think this is one he can win." Mrs. Coley had smiled, then glanced around, making sure no one stood near enough to hear. "I say it's about time he stood up to his father and proved he's a man."

Sam had only nodded, but she'd mulled the housekeeper's words over as she hurried toward Jen's house.

Was that what Ryan was doing? Proving himself to his father? If so, that might explain why he wanted to do this all on his own. She'd have to think about that, but first she wanted to talk to Jen.

But when Lila opened the door, her voice was hushed. "I'm sorry, Sam, but she's napping. Here, let me take those," Lila had said, taking the assignment sheets from Sam. "Even though her sleeping schedule is all twisted around, I just can't make myself wake her," Jen's mom apologized. "But here's yesterday's homework."

"Well, please tell her to call me. I'm going out riding," Sam paused, but explaining Pam had seemed too complicated a message to leave with Jen's mom. "But I'll be back home for dinner. And I really want to talk to her."

"I'll tell her," Lila had said, but then she'd taken a quick look around and added, "You won't be doing this much longer. I'm making headway with Jen's dad."

Now, Ace shifted impatiently beneath Sam. He tossed his head as high as the reins would allow, then pawed the dirt. He didn't move toward the water, because he wasn't thirsty, but he was bored.

"Okay, boy," Sam said. "Let's go find Pam."

When she just kept sitting there, Ace swung his head around. For a second, his brown eyes met hers, then he concentrated on the toe of her boot.

Sure, it had been over a year since she'd seen her friend from California, but Sam knew she'd recognize her. So why was she feeling shy?

Pam and Sam. Kids at school had joked about their rhyming names, but neither of them cared. It had suited their tight friendship.

The two of them had spent hundreds of hours in each other's apartments on the same San Francisco street, more at basketball practice and games. And, Sam thought, if she added in the many movies and museums they'd gone to, they might as well have lived in the same family.

Sam's fingers toyed with the horsehair bracelet on her left wrist. Woven of the Phantom's hair, it usually comforted her, but today its magic didn't work. She should feel better, since she'd seen the Phantom just that morning, but seeing him had only made her long for the stallion more.

"There they are, Ace," Sam said.

Near the mouth of Lost Canyon, Sam caught a flash of something so bright, she squinted against the shine.

She lifted her reins and wheeled Ace around. Sam touched her heels to the gelding's sides and leaned forward in the saddle. As the bay took off, Sam's brown Stetson flew back on its stampede string and she was smiling into the wind, leaving her shyness behind.

Chapter Seven ⟫

ℱor over a century, the legend said, Lost Canyon had been haunted by the ghosts of murdered Indian ponies. But the sounds echoing from its high stone walls as Sam and Pam greeted each other must have cheered even those sad spirits.

"Pam!" Sam shouted. In her hurry, her boot twisted in her stirrup. If Ace hadn't been such a good horse, she might have fallen. But he was and she didn't. The little mustang stood ground-tied as Sam rushed at her old friend.

Somehow they managed to hug, talk, and jump up and down at the same time.

"Your hair's long again!" Pam said, shaking Sam by the shoulders.

"Oh my gosh, you're so much taller!" Sam said, tilting her head back as if it were the only way she could see up to Pam's face.

"Giraffe girl, that's me," Pam laughed. "Wow, you only come up to my collarbone! How funny is that!"

"But you look just the same," Sam said with satisfaction. She stepped back to take in Pam's appearance. Though a twisted red bandanna held her cap of brown hair away from her face, it still sprang out in the every-which-way curls Sam remembered. Pam's green eyes and freckles were the same, too.

"You, too, except . . ." Pam licked her lips and tilted her head to one side. "There's something different. You look older. No, that's not it, but kind of . . ."

"Capable."

Both girls turned to face Pam's mother.

Dr. Mora O'Malley had the same green eyes and brown hair as her daughter, but her hair was wound into a no-nonsense knot at the back of her head, thick glasses magnified her eyes, and she handled her height like a model.

"Yeah, that's it," Pam agreed. "You do look kind of in charge."

Sam shook her head. "It must be the boots," she said, stomping to displace some of their dust coating. "Or maybe the muscles I'm getting from all the chores I have to do on the ranch."

"'On the ranch,' can you believe it?" Pam crowed as she squeezed Sam's shoulders again. "You always talked about the ranch, your dad, the horses and stuff, but now you actually live there. I can't picture it."

"You don't have to. You can come over and see it with your own eyes," Sam said.

"That would be cool," Pam said, and even though she nodded, Sam caught Pam's eyes darting toward Ace. "Maybe Mom can drive me over while she's doing her research."

"We could ride double on Ace," Sam teased.

"Pamela, you really should take this opportunity to learn to ride, if Sam's willing to teach you," Dr. Mora said.

"Sure," Sam began. She'd already begun wondering which horse Pam should use when her friend interrupted.

"We won't have time. Sam's in school until three?" She looked at Sam for a nod. "What we need is to catch up on each other's lives, Mom. You can't do that on a horse." Sam didn't have time to point out they could talk and ride at the same time, before Pam went on.

"Not when Sam would have to be giving me remedial lessons so I wouldn't fall off. But we could shoot a few baskets and talk at the same time."

"Can you believe we don't have a basketball hoop at the ranch? I didn't have anyone to play with, so I just—" Sam shrugged.

Basketball had been such a big part of her life in San Francisco, it was hard to believe she'd abandoned the sport. In San Francisco, she'd persuaded

Aunt Sue to let her and Pam mount a basketball hoop on her narrow garage, even though her short driveways led over a sidewalk and into the city street.

"No big deal," Pam said. She looked up at the soaring rock walls, then down at War Drum Flats before gazing at the endless blue sky. "You really live in this place."

This magical place, Sam thought as she looked up, too. For a minute, she felt as if she'd been towed aloft by a balloon. She was floating, sighing with pride at the beauty surrounding them.

"There's nothing out here," Pam went on.

Sam felt as if someone had shot the balloon she'd clung to, and she hit the ground with a bump. She almost launched into a lecture about the wildlife and plants Pam was too blind to see, but then she stopped.

"I love it," Sam said.

"And so do I."

Sam smiled gratefully at Pam's mother, whom she'd always called Dr. Mora, instead of Dr. O'Malley.

"It's beautiful country," Dr. Mora said with a slightly reproachful glance at her daughter. "An oasis for the soul."

Pam's eyelashes lowered. She jammed her hands into her pockets, then looked bashfully at Sam.

"I guess it does take some getting used to," Sam said.

"Well if you love it, I bet I will, too." Pam slipped

her arm through Sam's. "In fact, it's already coming to me."

Sam gave a skeptical smile.

"No, really. It's pretty, but in a bleak kind of way," Pam insisted. "Wide open, and so big, it's kind of overwhelming and scary."

"Not as scary as *some things*," Sam said. One city experience had become the yardstick by which they measured fright. She wondered if Pam remembered.

"Like Chinese New Year?" Pam asked.

"Exactly," Sam said.

Their eyes met in the memory of a night when they'd gotten separated from Aunt Sue and Pam's mom. Squealing in mock terror at a line of dragon dancers, they'd wiggled through the crowd watching the parade, darted by a vendor selling savory pork buns, and jogged past dozens of incense-scented shops. By the time they ended up in an alley where teenage guys were competing to see who could throw lighted firecrackers highest into the night sky, Sam and Pam were no longer pretending to be scared. They were lost and terrified.

After thirty minutes of searching, they followed directions from two little girls in kneesocks and school uniforms and crossed Grant Avenue to the worried adults. They'd been in big trouble. Their disappearance had gotten them grounded and restricted from television, the telephone, and each other for the rest of the weekend.

Sam shook her head. She remembered so much, and yet she almost felt as if she'd been a different person then.

Feeling a little shy, Sam leaned against Ace's shoulder. He ignored her for a patch of sun-dried grass.

Then Pam and her mother began lavishing him with pats.

"He's gorgeous," Pam said, running her hand over Ace's thick, glossy mane. "Do you brush his hair a hundred strokes every night?"

"You're going to make him conceited," Sam said, but she and Ace both stood taller at the admiration.

Watching her friend stroke Ace's red-gold shoulder, Sam saw Pam liked Ace, even if she was in no hurry to learn to ride. And that was okay.

"So, tell me again how you got to come out here," Sam asked as Ace drew a surprised laugh from Dr. Mora by licking her hand.

"I've been slicing apples," Dr. Mora said, and her smile remained as she began to talk about her work. "A small grant—"

"A grant is free money from some foundation or school," Pam broke in.

"Not exactly free. It pays my expenses while I work," Dr. Mora corrected. "Anyway, this grant was listed in one of my journals last year. It funds scholarly study of little known Native American legends that recur in diverse cultures."

Sam repeated the words silently in her mind. She must be out of practice from a summer off, because it took her a minute to process what Dr. Mora had just said.

Sam knew Pam's mother was a cultural anthropologist. Besides being a college professor, she studied ancient civilizations and their myths and folktales. She also wrote about them.

"You mean, you find different tribes in different places that tell the same stories?"

"Partly, but they don't have to be Native American tribes," Dr. Mora said. "For instance, there are tales of magical horses in Japan, Greece, Ireland . . ."

"I get it," Sam said. "And that's what you're studying? Magical horses?" Sam realized her mouth had opened in awe. "What a cool job!"

"I agree," Dr. Mora said. "I've been working on this paper for a while and I'm reaching the end of my research," Dr. O'Malley said, "but the chance to study Native American stories and compare them to what I've already found was tempting, so I applied."

"And, as usual, she won the grant," Pam said. She looked proud of her mother. Still, Sam knew Pam missed her mom when she traveled. More than once, she'd asked Sam to side with her, telling Dr. Mora she was gone too often for a single mother.

"I could become a juvenile delinquent," Pam had scolded her mother once, in front of Sam. But so far she hadn't, and Dr. Mora took Pam along on her research trips as often as she could.

Sam thought Pam actually had a pretty good deal.

"The legend that brought me here centers on an archetype that recurs throughout the West. Besides, it's a good chance to get you girls together."

"Isn't she the best?" Pam said. She gave her mother a one-armed hug and leaned her head against her shoulder.

"The best," Sam echoed. She felt a tug of longing for her own mother, though she'd lived most of her fourteen years without her.

Sam inhaled deeply and turned her attention to the O'Malleys' camp.

"This looks like home," Sam said. She noticed a rock ring around neatly stacked sticks, ready to kindle into a campfire. Sturdy chairs—three of them, Sam noticed with a smile—sat near the fire ring, granite boulders provided decoration, and a solar-powered shower was just a few steps away.

Though the truck had a camper shell, it was clear it only served as a place to sleep. Dr. Mora loved the outdoors, and her "living room" had the Nevada sky for a ceiling.

Sam noticed the red-and-white plastic cover tacked on a wooden table that held a cutting board, knife, sliced apples, stacked yellow plates, and a camp stove with something bubbling in an aluminum pot.

"We were hoping you'd arrive in time for dinner," Dr. Mora said.

"Well," Sam began hesitantly. "Gram knew I was coming out to find you, so I don't think she'd be surprised if I'm a little late getting back."

"Great," Pam said, but then she looked around. "How can you even tell how long it will take to get home from out here?"

Sam thought of tapping her watch, but there was no point in teasing Pam just because she was awed by the range. Sam couldn't forget how embarrassed she'd been when she'd first returned to Nevada and the cowboys joshed with her about the gaps in her Western wisdom.

"In a day, you'll start recognizing landmarks," Sam assured her friend. "It's no different from learning to get around with street signs."

"If you say so," Pam shook her head in disbelief.

Sam felt at home as she sat in the O'Malleys' extra chair, eating a simple dinner of vegetable stew over buckwheat noodles.

"Eat up." Dr. Mora nodded toward the plate of bread, cheese, and apples and added, "We've got plenty."

"That might be a good thing," Pam said as her eyes shifted to look over Sam's shoulder. "Is this like a favorite riding place?"

"Not really," Sam said, but Ace neighed a greeting just as Sam turned to follow Pam's gaze.

"I see him, too," Dr. Mora said. "He's been riding in from those salt flats almost since you arrived."

As Dr. Mora pointed, Sam spotted Ryan.

"It's a guy. Is he looking for you?" Pam asked in a teasing tone.

"It's Ryan. He lives on the ranch next to ours, but he's just the friend of a friend." Sam corrected Pam before she could get the wrong impression.

Sky Ranger approached at a flat-footed walk. He didn't sound winded, but Sam could tell Ryan had tapped the Thoroughbred's spare energy. This was the first time she'd seen the horse exhibit more obedience than spirit.

In fact, one of Dallas's expressions—"his get-up-and-go got up and went"—crossed Sam's mind. She hoped Ryan would ride a different horse for tomorrow's search.

"Is he a cowboy?" Pam whispered.

Sam almost pointed out the English saddle and lack of a cowboy hat. Instead, she said, "No, he's new here."

Pam looked interested.

"Hallo," Ryan greeted them, and when she heard his English accent, Pam looked even more intrigued. "I apologize for dropping in at dinnertime."

He could have ridden straight home instead of swerving from the trail that paralleled the highway, Sam thought. When she took in Ryan's dusty clothes and face, and the faint droop in his shoulders, she knew he was as tired as his horse and hoping for a break.

Dr. Mora didn't disappoint him.

"Nonsense," Dr. Mora said. "We're glad to have

you here." She was already up, getting Ryan a cup of water.

Sam was about to introduce everyone when Ryan dismounted and, still holding his reins, grabbed the cup. He gave a polite nod, but drained the cup before speaking.

"No sign of Hotspot," he said quickly to Sam. "But I did see two apparently wild horses. A chestnut and a bay, both stallions, trotting with quite a sense of purpose through the sagebrush."

Sam nodded, guessing he'd seen the bachelor stallions Mrs. Coley had named Spike and Yellow Tail. Before she explained that to Ryan and told Pam about Hotspot, her thoughts drew up short. Ryan's hands were shaking. She noticed it at the same time as Dr. Mora.

"Another cup of water?" Dr. Mora asked, taking the cup to refill.

"Yes, thank you," Ryan said. He flashed an embarrassed glance at Sam. "I fear I made a tenderfoot's mistake. I neglected to bring along a canteen, but I didn't want to waste time going back to the ranch for one."

"It's been a hundred degrees," Sam scolded. "Getting dehydrated, passing out, and having to run after your horse would have wasted a lot more—" Sam clapped a hand over her mouth when she saw Dr. Mora's amusement. "Oh my gosh, I sound like my dad."

The others laughed and Ryan admitted, "But you're right." Then, refreshed by his second cup of water, Ryan squared his shoulders and took in Pam and Dr. Mora with his smile. "I'm Ryan Slocum, heir to the Gold Dust Ranch, but more recently from Nottingham, England."

He'd charmed them both, Sam thought, and once Ryan had loosened Sky's girth, slipped his bit, and tied him to a stunted pinion pine, Ryan continued to win them over.

"I wouldn't think of evicting you from your chairs," he said when Dr. Mora tried to give him her seat. Instead, he sat carefully on a boulder. "But I will allow myself a taste of that wondrously aromatic dish you're cooking."

While he ate Dr. Mora's stew, Ryan explained how he'd come to be here. He told how he'd lived with his "mum" and become an accomplished equestrian, riding competitive jumpers, between taking rigorous courses at a British boarding school.

"Once I graduated, I decided to come to Nevada to spend time with my father and twin sister . . . yes, thank you, I will have a slice of bread. It looks lovely."

How did he manage to look so poised? Sam wondered. He balanced his cup and yellow tin plate, used the side of his plastic fork to cut a roly-poly red potato, *and* continued to conduct a conversation.

Sam decided it must be the sort of thing you

learned at boarding school, because she'd already dropped her spoon once and had to blow a bug off her bread. And she was sitting in a chair.

"Did your twin go to the same school in England?" Pam asked.

"No, Rachel's a year behind me. She's been schooled in the States," he said. When Sam pointedly cleared her throat, he added, "No cause-and-effect implied, of course. My sister's strongest interests do not lie in the classroom."

He could say *that* again. Rachel Slocum was more interested in makeup and MTV. Because she was her rich father's princess, she got everything she wanted, from a red sports car to a horse she'd never ridden. Now, her sights were set on a music career.

Ryan's expression dared Sam to say something critical about his twin, but Sam kept quiet.

Looking a little relieved, Ryan asked, "What brings you ladies to Lost Canyon?"

"I'm writing a paper about legendary horses. It's called 'From Sacrifice to Saint: Complementary Legends of the Wild Equid.' It may sound dry and academic," Dr. Mora said, "but it's not—"

"Of course not," Ryan said.

"—especially because I'm scouting contemporary sightings of a magical horse. It carries the sun on its back, bringing light to the world each morning—"

The plastic fork almost broke in Sam's grip. A horse haloed in morning sun floated across her memory.

"—stories told in places all over the world," Dr. Mora was continuing. "Some say it's a ghost whose only escape from darkness is at daybreak. Other tales claim it's a normal horse bewitched into the service of a sun god—"

Not magical. Not bewitched, Sam thought, just fleet and half wild.

"—one of the places where these stories recur is right here, around Lost Canyon," Dr. Mora finished with a nod.

As Ryan allowed his mannerly disbelief to break into words, Sam would bet she was the only one to catch his teasing look.

"And what do they call this creature?" he asked. "The Phantom Stallion?"

Any other day, Sam might have worried about the same thing, but not today. Her stallion wasn't the legendary horse Dr. Mora was describing.

"No," Dr. Mora said with a wave of her hand. "That's a separate legend altogether. This horse is generally thought of as a mare, like Epona in Britain. Unlike Epona, the white mare, this horse is parti-colored—dappled or spotted like the Chinese Tiger Horse—and she's called Dawn Runner."

Parti-colored, Sam thought. She almost nodded.

Dr. Mora sighed with pleasure and announced, "I have a meeting with a Shoshone tribal elder who saw this sun bearer in July."

That Shoshone elder could be Jake's grandfather,

Sam thought. He lived out near Monument Lake, but he drove back and forth to Three Ponies Ranch all the time. So it would make sense he'd seen her.

"Surely," Ryan began, and Sam could tell he was struggling to remain polite, "you aren't saying this miraculous horse exists?"

Dr. Mora's palms met and her fingers interlaced. "Legends are often born from the mingling of fact and longing. It will be a fascinating interview, if nothing else, since it's the most recent sighting in this century."

"No, it's not," Sam said without meaning to. "I saw the Dawn Runner just this morning."

Chapter Eight ❧

"She's joking," Pam explained in a tolerant tone reserved for friends who've gone slightly crazy.

"No, I'm not," Sam said. "Or, at least, not exactly. I *did* see a spotted mare running next to the La Charla River just as the sun was coming up."

"How exciting," Dr. Mora said.

"Indeed. I just wish you'd mentioned it before now," Ryan said. And then he yawned, covering his lips, too courteous to let them see.

"I thought of it, but she would have been long gone, Ryan. And she was headed toward the Blind Faith sanctuary, where you were going to look anyway," Sam insisted.

She didn't point out how stubborn he'd been

about capturing Hotspot on his own. That reminder might have started a fight, and this wasn't the time or the place for bickering.

"Wait a minute. I'm lost. So, did you already know about the legend?" Pam asked.

"No, we're talking about a real horse," Sam told her. "Her name is Apache Hotspot and she's Ryan's."

"And she was out running around by herself? I don't get it."

"Help me clear the dishes, and then we'll talk about it while we walk down to the lake. All right?" Dr. Mora said.

"Splendid," Ryan said. "I was hoping to locate a hiding place, rather like a hunting blind, where I could watch for Hotspot if she comes in for water."

It was only a comparison, Sam knew, but it made her uncomfortable when Ryan talked about a hunting blind—one of those camouflaged lookouts used by people with rifles—and Hotspot in the same sentence.

Cleanup was over and they were walking through the rangeland dusk when Dr. Mora noticed Sam's horsehair bracelet.

"Did you make it yourself?" she asked.

"Yes, it's hair from my stallion. Well, I call him mine, but he's really not anymore. When he was a foal, he was, but now he's wild."

"The horse you were riding when you had the accident," Dr. Mora said. "I remember." She glanced at the bracelet again. "Did you know that worldwide, more amulets and good-luck charms are made from horsehair than any other substance?"

"Really?" Sam asked.

"That's what I've read."

Sam was about to tell Dr. Mora the bracelet wasn't a good-luck charm, but since she wasn't sure exactly what it was, she didn't correct her.

"And speaking of foals, that's why I'm tracking Hotspot," Ryan said. "She became separated from her foal about a month ago. Now, he's not doing as well as he might, so I'm trying to bring her back to him."

That was certainly a cleaned-up version of the truth, Sam thought. But she kept walking, enjoying Pam's companionship instead of confiding the ugly details of Ryan tricking her into hiding Hotspot and Shy Boots, then leaving her to take the blame for stealing them.

Sam felt a secretive smile play over her lips and had to admit to herself that even though she didn't want to ruin the tranquil mood now, she might not be able to resist gossiping with Pam a little later.

"So, will your sister look after your colt while you're searching for Hotspot?" Pam asked.

"Not in this lifetime," Sam muttered.

"Samantha doesn't hold a very high opinion of my sister," Ryan said, and though the words were critical, his tone wasn't.

And that makes me look bad, Sam thought, but it

took a few seconds for her to figure out how to contradict him without lying.

"Rachel and Ryan have just been brought up differently from me," Sam said.

"With money," Ryan put in, then laughed, and despite his fine manners, Sam knew Dr. Mora and Pam didn't like the entitled way in which he said it.

Although they walked a quiet lap around the desert watering hole, they concluded what Sam had known from the start. This was a safe place for mustangs to drink because there were no nearby hiding places.

"This won't work," Ryan said with a disgusted shake of his head.

"You could set up camp here," Dr. Mora recommended. "I have a friend who's a wildlife biologist and he insists you don't see anything until you become part of the animal's environment."

"I don't want to study her," Ryan said as they turned to walk back toward the O'Malleys' camp. "I want to trap her."

Did Ryan hear the uneasy silence between their footfalls as they walked back? If so, he didn't say anything. But Sam noticed, and a single glimpse from the corner of her eye told her Dr. Mora did, too. She was sizing up Ryan as if he were under a microscope.

Ace's nicker reminded Sam that she would have to ride home in full darkness. The trail was clear and she and Ace knew it well, but she'd be testing her family's patience, especially on a school night.

"I'd better get going," Sam said reluctantly.

Dr. Mora had asked Pam to light the kindling arranged in the rock ring. Now the cozy campfire smell made Sam want to stay.

"How about using my satellite phone to call home and see if you can stay just a little longer?" Dr. Mora said.

When she began burrowing in her box of supplies, Sam wondered why Pam's mom had buried her phone in the clutter. But she hadn't.

Mora lifted a plastic bag out of the box and swung it like a lure.

"I have marshmallows for toasting," she said in a tempting tone.

Sam didn't even pretend to resist, but she held her breath as she dialed home. When Dad answered on the first ring, she was afraid she was already in trouble. Since she couldn't talk and hold her breath at the same time, she crossed her fingers instead.

"Dad?" Sam asked, then closed her eyes tight. "I'm with Pam and Dr. Mora. Ryan Slocum is here, too, and I want to know if I can stay just a little longer before I start riding back."

"Where's 'here'?" Dad asked.

"Oh, we're about midway between War Drum Flats and Lost Canyon. Um, a little closer to the mouth of Lost Canyon."

Sam waited.

"You'll have to ride most of the way in the dark," Dad said.

"Yeah, but I'm on Ace. We know the way home."

"You have homework?"

"I don't. None."

"Okay. Don't suppose it will be any darker if you leave in twenty minutes than if you leave right now. No galloping. Even a savvy pony can misjudge his footing in the dark."

"I'll be careful," Sam promised.

Dad cleared his throat. "Your Gram wants to know if you've eaten."

"I had dinner with Pam and her mom," Sam said, and then, since she knew Gram would be curious, she added, "We had stew, bread, and apples."

"And cheese," Pam put in, and Sam opened her eyes to see her friend fidgeting in front of her.

Dad must have heard Pam, too, because he gave a quiet laugh.

"Okay, then. Porch light will be on. Me and Blaze will be waitin'."

"Thanks, Daddy!" she said, and then punched the button to turn the phone off.

"Yay!" Pam cheered, then celebrated by handing Sam a stick with a knife-sharpened point.

Before she took it, she followed Dr. Mora's nod and offered the phone to Ryan.

"No thanks," Ryan said.

"Are you sure?"

"Absolutely," he said.

Sam shrugged.

Ryan turned down the chance to roast marshmallows, too, after asking, "Just curious, but do you have any metal toasting forks?"

When Pam said no, Ryan claimed he really couldn't eat another bite.

As Sam eased a plump, white marshmallow onto her stick, she guessed Ryan had a right to be fastidious. True, the sticks weren't sanitary, but wouldn't ramming them into the flames kill germs?

As she squatted near the campfire and practiced her turn-and-burn roasting technique, Sam couldn't shake off the feeling that she'd forgotten something she was supposed to do tonight. She'd told Dad the truth. She didn't have any homework, but the memory of some other responsibility hovered just out of reach.

"I don't know how you can eat them like that," Pam said as Sam withdrew her flaming dessert from the fire.

Sam stood up, stepped back from the campfire's heat, and pulled the black crust off her marshmallow. She popped it into her mouth, then returned to her position by the fire and thrust the goo that remained on her stick back into the flames.

"This way, I get to eat them twice," she explained.

"Why would one want to consume charcoal even once?" Ryan asked, watching the orange tongues of fire lick at the sizzling marshmallow.

"It's delicious, but I bet you're the kind of guy who turns your marshmallow way above the fire, one millimeter at a time," Sam accused.

"Of course not," Ryan said. "They're only a perfect golden brown if you turn them one *half* millimeter at a time."

They laughed, and suddenly, Sam remembered something she'd been meaning to ask Dr. Mora.

"You said the name of your paper was something like, 'From Sacrifice to Saints.' What does that mean?"

"It's a little gruesome," Dr. Mora warned. She glanced toward Sky and Ace, dipped her head in silent apology, then defended the ancient people she was studying. "In primitive times, it was pretty common to offer a prized animal as a gift to the gods."

"I know I'm going to be sorry I asked, but by 'offer' you mean . . . ?" Sam swallowed hard, then waited.

Before her mother answered, Pam grimaced and made a slashing motion across her throat.

"They killed them? Not really," Sam said.

"I'm afraid so," Dr. Mora confirmed. "I know you've heard of civilizations that believed in sacrificing to their gods. The Romans killed white birds, bulls, and other flawless creatures. Mayans trusted human sacrifice. Some Celtic horse cultures gave their fastest, most beautiful stallions a life of luxury before they sacrificed them."

"And some even ate them," Pam said, shuddering. "I've read the rough draft of Mom's paper."

"But why did they do that?" Sam asked.

Dr. Mora used her index fingers to reposition her glasses before she explained. "We think they were asking higher powers to protect them from plague, drought, flood, and poor crops—sacrificing what they held dear to save their own lives."

Sam gazed around her. Firelight flared on Ryan's dirt-smudged face and disheveled hair. Shadows shifted to show Pam's green eyes glowing from beneath the bandanna that had slipped down her brow. Then Sam looked at her own pointed roasting stick. Thousands of years ago, they might have been gathered around this desert campfire for much different reasons.

She stared over at Ace and Sky. Both geldings' eyes glowed red with firelight.

"Some say horses remember, and that's why they don't entirely trust us," Dr. Mora said.

"What is it they're supposed to remember?" Ryan's question sounded dubious.

"When they were food, beasts of burden, and sacrifices," Dr. Mora said. "Some think that explains why a domestic horse sometimes resists capture, even by a person he knows. It's that primal memory. They probably don't understand it any more than we do our own primal memories. For example, you know how uneasy we humans feel at a sudden silence?"

When the very word *silence* made all four of them quiet, they laughed.

"Why do we feel that way?" Pam asked.

"Theories vary, but one says that before we developed big enough brains to be predators, we were nothing but thin-skinned, short-clawed," — Dr. Mora held up her fingernails — "dull-toothed prey. When birds stopped calling to each other and a sudden quiet fell over ancient forests, that meant a predator was prowling for dinner. But that was long ago. Horses' memories are from more recent times. Some horse bones marked by human teeth have been dated at hundreds, not thousands, of years old."

The thought sickened Sam. She stared toward Ace. The bay gelding stood motionless, almost as if he understood this conversation about her ancestors sitting around a fire like this one, gnawing on horse bones.

Chills prickled down Sam's arms. She put down her stick, pushed up from her squatting position near the fire, and went to hug Ace.

"Don't listen, boy," she told him, but she was pretty sure Ace wouldn't be the one having nightmares about blood spilling from a beautiful stallion.

Apparently Ryan's mind had circled back to that awful image, too.

"That's puzzling," he said. "Sacrificing the best, I mean. Not a sensible way to build up good blood lines."

"No," Dr. Mora agreed. "But I suppose everyone

understands that some things are supposed to be unattainable, and never possessed. . . ."

Sam was nodding, thinking how she wanted the Phantom to remain free, even though she could have built a case for reclaiming him.

"Not my father," Ryan said. "He believes everything has a value in dollars and cents and it's his right to buy it, even—"

Ryan's square jaw slammed closed. He stopped talking so suddenly, it sounded as if someone had flipped a switch. He shook his head.

"Pardon me," he said. "That was totally out of line."

"No big deal," Sam said.

Pam chimed in, telling Ryan she didn't care, either.

Then Dr. Mora added, "I guess it all boils down to what the wise man said."

"Go ahead, Mom. We're waiting," Pam coaxed.

Dr. Mora cleared her throat melodramatically, then recited, "Not everything that counts can be counted and not everything that can be counted counts."

"Wow," Sam said. "I love that! Is it a Native American saying? Or—I know—the Dalai Lama?"

"Actually, it's from Albert Einstein," Dr. Mora said.

"No way," Sam said, but Dr. Mora nodded.

Sam couldn't believe it. Someone she'd banished to the part of her brain reserved for boring mathematics had said something so perfect.

She'd have to remember to tell Jen. Her friend was a fan of Einstein. She even had a black-and-white poster of a static-haired Einstein on her bedroom wall.

All at once, as if a bell had tolled, Sam realized Dr. Mora's tales had made her forget the time. She hoped her professors were this fascinating when she got to college. Right now, though, she had other things to worry about.

It had been more than twenty minutes since she'd talked to Dad.

"I'm going to be so late," Sam gasped.

This time Dr. Mora didn't beg her to stay. Pam's mom sat at the fireside, talking to Ryan as Pam watched Sam saddle up.

Sam had bent to draw Ace's cinch snug when Pam leaned over and whispered, "Is he your boyfriend?"

Sam bumped her head on her stirrup as she jerked back.

"Ryan? No! Are you crazy?" Sam hissed.

"Relax. You're scaring pretty Ace," Pam said. She patted the gelding's neck as Sam moved around to slip his bit back into his mouth. Pam sounded gently sarcastic as she added, "I don't know what I could have been thinking. He's cute, smart, likes horses the same way you do—" Pam broke off to shake her head. "I can see where that would be totally repulsive."

Sam glared toward Ryan. Maybe looking at him through Pam's eyes, it was all true.

"When you get to know him, he's not—" Sam stopped, remembering Ryan's devotion to Shy Boots and his vow to *cowboy up.* "I guess he's trying."

"Trying to do what?"

Ace's front hooves shifted restlessly.

Sam imagined her brain doing the same thing. She didn't know how to explain Ryan. "Let's just say that if I were going to have a boyfriend, I'd pick someone more loyal and trustworthy."

"That sounds more like a dog than a guy," Pam said, but she was laughing.

"Isn't *that* sad!" Sam giggled as she swung into the saddle.

"I'll jog along with you for a minute, okay?" Pam asked.

"Sure," Sam said. After all, Dad had told her to ride carefully. "And Ryan's also my friend Jen's boyfriend. Sort of."

"Oh, yeah," Pam said, planting words between breaths as she trotted alongside Ace. "That could be sticky."

"Hey! How long will you be here? Do you want to do something tomorrow?"

"I want to, but it depends on Mom. As soon as she gets what she needs, we could be driving away, but my classes don't start for two more weeks and she *did* say I could see if your school would give me a visitor's pass," Pam said, beginning to pant.

"That would be so cool!" Sam crowed. "I'd love for you to meet the kids on the newspaper staff. And even though she isn't at school right now, I'm taking Jen homework every day after school, so you can meet her. You'll love her, Pam. Jen is so smart and funny." Sam noticed Pam's lopsided smile. Did that mean she'd hurt Pam's feelings? "She's my best friend *here*," Sam clarified.

Even as the words came out of her mouth, Sam suddenly knew what she'd been trying to remember all night. She'd asked Lila to have Jen call when she woke up. She'd promised to be home in time for dinner. Sam glanced down at the glowing numbers on her watch.

Eight thirty-seven. Neither Jen's family nor hers appreciated phone calls after nine o'clock, and she'd be riding for close to an hour. Even if it got her in trouble, Sam knew she had to call Jen the minute she got in.

"Hey," Pam said, her voice trailing off as her steps slowed. "I can tell you really need to get going. I'll see if I can come to your school tomorrow," she called. "If you don't see me —"

"I'll ride back out here," Sam shouted back, and then she waved.

"Okay, boy," Sam muttered to Ace as the distance grew between them and Pam, "we're not doing anything stupid, but I know a little shortcut across the shallow end of the lake on War Drum Flats, and we're going to take it."

Chapter Nine ❧

"**H**ey, knock that off!" Sam snapped at her horse.

Frisky from his long rest at the O'Malleys' camp, Ace humped his back up to buck.

Dark rangelands stretched around her for what looked like hundreds of miles and now, as she twisted in her saddle, even the orange eye of the campfire had disappeared behind a rock outcropping.

She did not want to get stranded out here. Sure, she could shout for help and maybe, if she was lucky, someone would hear, but rescue wasn't in her plans for the night.

For one thing, it would take too long, and she had to get home and call Jen. That's why she was taking this shortcut Ace was protesting.

"You like the water, remember?" she crooned to her horse.

Sam felt him relax, responding to her gentle tone. She lowered her rein hand, rewarding him for his calm continuation into the lake.

"Good boy," she said as one hoof, then another plopped down, and they cut across the shallow end of the lake instead of following the half-moon-shaped shore.

The problem with mustangs, Sam decided, was that they made their own decisions once they had full bellies. In the wild, they responded with speed to all the sights, sounds, and smells that signaled danger. But Ace didn't understand that she had a good reason for asking him to get his feet wet, and he was letting her know it was a bad idea.

A breeze blew over the lake, bringing the smell of hot rocks and damp vegetation. Sam shivered a little, wishing she'd tied a sweatshirt behind her cantle. It had been so hot this afternoon, she hadn't thought of it, and that was stupid.

While she was kicking herself for being unprepared, Ace stopped and stared toward the middle of the lake.

His intent stare gave Sam chills that had nothing to do with the wind. All alone on the range, with Ace knee-deep in this desert lake, she thought of Water Babies.

"Now *I'm* the one who needs to knock it off," she said out loud to Ace. "I know this lake. It doesn't have Water Babies. Besides, I've seen mustangs drinking and playing here."

Ace's head bobbed and his mane flapped as he gave a loud snort.

"That's right," she said, agreeing with her horse. "They don't exist."

Sam drew in a shivery breath and blamed Dr. Mora's ancient tales for turning her mind to horror stories out of the past.

Water Babies sounded sweet and chubby, but the Native American legends were bloodcurdling, at least to her.

The little lake dwellers swam unseen in the depths of desert lakes, only coming ashore to switch places with human babies left unattended. For the first time, Sam wondered what became of the real babies. All she knew was that the changelings surprised their unsuspecting parents with long, needlelike teeth.

Dr. Mora said the Dawn Runner story was a mixture of truth and longing, but Sam would bet Water Babies had been made up as a cautionary tale to make parents keep watch over their babies while they were at the water's edge.

A coyote's howl drifted from the foothills. Ace's ears twitched, but he kept moving steadily toward the shore ahead.

Could Water Babies scull along in the shallows,

tummies touching the lake bottom, searching for something to bite? Sam looked around her. She knew those ripples were from Ace's movements. Absolutely. But what if they weren't? What if Water Babies liked to sink their sharp teeth into horses' pasterns?

You are scaring yourself, Sam thought.

"We're almost across," Sam comforted Ace, but he must have heard something worrisome in her voice.

The mustang's head came up. He raised his knees in a high-stepping prance, leaving his hooves in the water as short a time as possible, and then he broke into a splashing trot.

Sam didn't stop him. In fact, she shifted her weight forward. They hit the shore at a solid lope that lasted all the way home.

Dad stood in the golden glow of the porch light. In jeans and an untucked shirt, he looked ready for bed and his voice was a little cranky.

"'Bout time," he said as Sam slowed Ace to a walk.

She stopped the gelding in front of the porch.

"I know," Sam said. "Sorry."

Ace blew a loud breath through his nostrils.

"Give that horse a good rubdown, then get yourself inside. Might as well phone Jen, too, before she calls and wakes up the whole house again."

"Okay, Dad," Sam said, but she was wincing.

Tonight's tardiness could mess up her chances for

hanging out with Pam while she was here, but Dad hadn't said anything about that.

"'Night, Dad," she said, and he turned toward the front door, but then he stopped.

"Have a good time talkin' with Pam and her mom, did ya?"

"I did! It was great to see them. Pam's just the same and her mom is so cool."

Dad nodded. He didn't say anything, but Sam wondered if he was thinking of the two years she'd spent in San Francisco with Aunt Sue and Pam and Dr. Mora. According to Brynna, those had been long, lonely months for Dad.

"Sunrise is gonna come mighty early," Dad said, and then he went inside.

At last Ace was bedded down for the night. Sam's boots felt heavy as she walked across the ranch yard. She kept sighing for no particular reason. She guessed she was just tired.

She could almost feel her cheek settling against her pillow, but first she had to call Jen.

Cougar jumped down from a kitchen chair where he'd been curled up, and rubbed against Sam's leg. When she reached down to pet him, he reached up and hooked his front claws into her jeans and stretched the long striped length of his feline body.

"Ow," Sam complained, but the cat's claws had

barely pricked her, so she let him settle on her lap as she claimed the chair he'd been sleeping on. Sighing again, Sam muttered, "Please let Jen be sitting right by the phone."

She already knew it was late. She didn't want to discuss *how* late with one of Jen's parents.

Jen picked up the phone in the middle of the first ring.

"Hello?"

"Hi. I am so sorry I got home late," Sam apologized.

"I guess you had a lot to talk about with your friend Pam from San Francisco," Jen said.

Her voice wasn't mean or jealous. In fact, it was nearly expressionless.

"How did you know?" Sam blurted.

Wrong, wrong, wrong. Sam tilted her head back and stared toward the ceiling as if she could suck the words back into her mouth. That sounded like she'd been trying to keep Pam a secret.

"Your Gram told me during one of our short but frequent conversations tonight," Jen said. "I hope I didn't get you in trouble by calling so much."

"No." Sam stared toward the door to the living room as if she could see through it, up the stairs to Gram's bedroom and into her sleeping mind. "At least, I don't think so." Sam sighed again. "I just found out Pam was going to be here. She and her mom are camped out by Lost Canyon, and her mom's doing some research about Native American legends. I was going to tell you about everything this afternoon, but when I got there, you were asleep."

"I know," Jen said. "I don't really care."

"I'm sorry, though," Sam said. She waited for Jen to say something else, but all she heard was the hum of the refrigerator and Cougar's purr.

"If I'm jealous at all," Jen said, "it's because I can't go riding with you and Ryan."

"I hate that," Sam said.

"Good." Jen sounded satisfied, until she added, "He hasn't come back yet, by the way."

"Really? Well, he was still talking to Pam's mom when I rode off," Sam said.

"To Pam's mom," Jen repeated.

"Yeah, he seemed interested in the research she's doing."

"Still, I wish you hadn't left him there," Jen said. "I know he's a big boy . . ."

Was Jen really blaming her for letting Ryan ride home alone? Or was Jen worried that Ryan would be distracted by a girl she didn't even know?

Sam only had a defense for the first part, so she used it.

"Ryan's an excellent rider," Sam interrupted. "Lots better than me, and you know it."

"Except you know what you're doing out on the range," Jen pointed out. "And he doesn't."

"Maybe," Sam agreed, as she thought of Ryan

being without water all day long.

Then she looked up. Someone upstairs was moving around. She might not be in trouble yet, but she had a feeling she was headed in that direction.

"Did you have fun?" Jen asked.

"I did," Sam admitted. Then she began talking fast. "Mostly we listened to Dr. Mora—that's Pam's mom—talk about horse legends, and one of them—oh yeah, I need to tell you about this tomorrow."

"Why not now?" Jen moaned.

"Because I think someone's coming downstairs to yell at me."

"But Pam—" Jen started.

"She's really nice and you'll get to meet her because she's probably going to get a visitor's pass and hang out with me at school."

Great. What a wonderful friend you are, Sam scolded herself. *Is there anything else Jen wants more than to go back to school? And not only are you going, but your old best friend is going with you? Nice.*

"I hate her already," Jen said, but she was clearly joking. "She's probably gorgeous, too, and Ryan—"

"—didn't even look at her. She's a jock and taller than he is," Sam said.

"Okay then, you're saying I only have to worry about the mom?"

"Jen!" Sam shrieked.

It was then she heard a throat clearing from the stairs. It sounded like Brynna.

"Jen," Sam whispered. "They're only here for a few days. You have nothing to worry about. Now, I have to get off. Really."

"Okay," Jen said, and even though the word wavered with indecision, Sam gently hung up.

"So she didn't show up at school?" Jen asked the next day.

Sam was still sitting in the backseat of the Slocums' blue Mercedes when she heard Jen's question through the open car window. She'd spotted her friend as soon as the car pulled through Gold Dust Ranch's iron gates.

She knew Jen was talking about Pam, but she hadn't even gathered her books and Jen's yet. She did that and unsnapped her seat belt. She drew a breath to answer as Jen opened the car door.

"Did they refuse to let her visit this early in the year or what?" Jen chattered as if she'd been cut off from school for months instead of days.

"I don't think so," Sam said, but Jen had switched her attention to Rachel.

"Hi, Rachel," Jen said.

The rich girl's lips, glossed a bright shade of nectarine, parted in disbelief. "Hello?"

Sam didn't know if Rachel was recoiling from Jen's friendliness or the retina-searing green of her T-shirt and matching pom-poms holding the ends of her braids.

"Don't mind me," Jen joked. "I have cabin fever. I'll talk to anyone."

Sam couldn't decide whether to gasp or laugh at Rachel's expression. So she just slipped out of the backseat and followed Jen toward Shy Boots's empty paddock.

"Where are they?" Sam asked.

"In the small pasture," Jen said. "My dad decided to move them to where they'd have more room."

As they watched Princess Kitty and Shy Boots, Jen babbled.

"My dad went over the pasture like a maniac this morning, making sure there's nothing Boots could eat that could contribute to him feeling bad. I mean, having Kitty in there with him is starting to help, I think, but it hasn't been like magic."

Even as she said that, Princess Kitty, gleaming red-gold in the September sun, approached the foal. Shy Boots raised his head and his ears flicked toward her.

"Jen, you might not see it because you've been watching them so much, but to me, he already looks better. Watch—he's trying to figure out what she wants."

Princess Kitty definitely wanted something. She faced the colt and looked into his eyes. He tossed his head, trying to avoid her gaze, but he didn't move away from her.

"Dad even ran the harrow over the pasture," Jen said, "breaking up all the old horse manure that I somehow missed with my rake, and plowing it under in case there were parasites in it."

Together, they watched Princess Kitty move closer to Shy Boots until they stood neck to neck, facing opposite directions.

"I get it," Sam said quietly, nodding at the horses.

A smile claimed Jen's face as she understood, too. "She's teaching him how horses groom each other."

Princess Kitty sniffed the colt's cocoa-brown neck. When he trembled but didn't move away, she nuzzled it with her lips. Wide-eyed, the little Appaloosa accepted the mare's touch.

Kitty stood beside Shy Boots for several minutes. While Jen kept talking about her dad, Kitty seemed to be waiting for the tension to leave the muscles holding up the colt's high-flung head.

Finally, he lowered his head and the mare gave Shy Boots a series of short, firm bites on his neck. He didn't move off. In fact, the colt looked mesmerized. His eyelids drooped as if he were receiving a massage.

"He's learning," Sam said. "Soon, I bet he'll be grooming her back."

"I hope so," Jen said. "But wait, you have to keep listening about my dad, because after he cleaned that entire pasture, he had this long talk with Linc about hiring at least one permanent hand, and well—here's what I'm trying to figure out." Jen stopped and watched Sam.

"Yeah?" Sam prompted.

"Is he feeling guilty over seeing Princess Kitty

with Shy Boots? You know, because she lost that one foal and he sold the other? Or is he trying to get the ranch in good shape for some reason, like it's going to be sold? Or is he just avoiding me and Mom so we won't harass him about school?"

"I'm totally mixed up," Sam admitted. "What are you talking about?"

"I don't know," Jen said. "Watching my dad and trying to figure out what he's thinking about school is driving me nuts."

Sam shrugged. "Maybe he's not thinking about you or school at all. Maybe he's just working as hard as he can because he doesn't have much help, and that's why he's talking to Linc."

"Maybe," Jen said.

Gold Dust Ranch's iron gate clanged open, and Gram's yellow Buick drove in.

"Were you expecting her so soon?" Jen asked.

"No, she wasn't supposed to leave until I called," Sam said. Her heart raced. Was something wrong? What if Brynna had gone into premature labor, or—

Just then, she noticed a flurry of curly hair in the passenger's seat.

"That's Pam!" Sam said.

"Cool," Jen said, but she didn't sound as if she meant it.

Searching her mind for a way to make Jen feel better, Sam said, "I don't know why Gram would just drop in with—"

"You're joking, right?" Jen asked. "This isn't the

most formal place in the world. No reservations required. Of course your grandmother can drop in with your friend. Get a grip, Sam."

"Thanks," Sam said. She exhaled loudly.

When Pam climbed out of Gram's car, she wore a determined expression much like Jen's.

"Hi," Pam said quietly. Her arms stayed at her sides, but one hand flipped back and forth in a wave.

Even though she was nearly six feet tall and looked totally athletic in roomy black shorts and a trim jersey, Pam ducked her head, appearing shy.

"Hi," Jen responded.

Sam was about to introduce the two, when Gram called to her from inside the car.

"When Pam and her mom stopped by the ranch at the same time I was heading into Darton, I decided to bring her on by. I figured you wouldn't mind spending some time together," Gram called across the front seat. "I'll be back in a couple of hours."

"Thanks, Gram," Sam said. Then, as Gram drove off, Sam said, "So, anyway . . ." She paused as her throat tightened.

Was there an order in which you were supposed to introduce people? Like oldest first? But they were all the same age. And did it mean anything if she introduced Pam to Jen first? Or Jen to Pam?

"I'm Jen Kenworthy—"

"I'm Pam O'Malley—"

The girls' words collided. They laughed awkwardly.

Then Jen leaned forward with her arm outstretched for a handshake.

"I'm not always this thick around the middle. I broke a rib and I'm all wrapped up in bandages."

Pam answered, "That must be nice in this heat."

Pam was usually good at putting people at ease, but now all three of them just stood there.

"So, my mom got everything worked out for a visitor's pass to your school." Pam's gesture included both Jen and Sam. "And I was thinking maybe I'd drive tomorrow."

"What?" Sam yelped. "The driving age here is sixteen, just like it is in California."

"But I know how to drive," Pam said. "And even though Mom doesn't let me do it in the city, sometimes in desolate areas, she loans me the truck and I can go off on my own."

Desolate areas. When Pam said it, Sam felt a sting. She didn't know why, but she could tell she wasn't alone. Behind Jen's glasses, she looked startled, too.

"Compared to San Francisco, there's not much traffic," Sam said, making an excuse. Then, she turned toward Pam. "But we do have a sheriff, and he enforces traffic laws."

"I love it!" Pam said, smiling. "Not a regular cop, but a sheriff."

Was Pam visualizing a bowlegged Western movie sheriff with a tin star pinned to his vest and a six-gun holstered on his hip?

"He's just like a regular cop," Sam said.

Pam nodded. The fingers on one hand plucked at her crazy curls.

Jen looked down and watched the wiggling of her toes, visible even inside her leather tennis shoes.

"Is the baby of Ryan's horse here?" Pam asked. "Do you think I could see it?"

"Sure," Sam said. Pam was a genius to think of horses, the best and most comfortable topic in the world. "His name is Shy Boots and he's right over here. Jen's been watching over him while Ryan's out searching for Hotspot, the mom."

Sam had only taken two steps toward the small pasture when she noticed Jen wasn't following.

"I know," Jen said as Sam looked back. "Why don't I go get us some lemonade and something to eat, while you two look at the horses? I'll meet you on the porch in a couple of minutes."

"That'd be great," Sam said. "Thanks, Jen."

"You're welcome, Sam," Jen said, and her gracious tone hinted that Sam was overdoing the politeness.

Maybe the scent of a stranger had carried to the horses' sensitive nostrils, or maybe they were tired of being watched. In any case, Shy Boots stood against the farthest fence. With Princess Kitty standing in front of him, all Pam could see of the foal was his long brown legs.

"This is an incredible ranch," Pam said.

"Yeah, the guy who owns it is a multimillionaire," Sam said, then added, "Ryan's dad."

"Right," Pam said. "The man who thinks everything's for sale."

Sam nodded, smiling.

"Jen seems nice. What does she call those little things in her hair? Deely-boppers or doodads or something? Are they, uh, fashionable here?"

Maybe Pam didn't mean to sound rude, but she did, and Sam didn't think it was a coincidence that Jen wasn't here to hear the question. Sam just shrugged.

And when she left Pam outside to wander around looking at things and made her way back to the foreman's house, Sam heard Jen talking with her mother.

Lila said, "It's hard to believe she's from San Francisco. She looks just like the girl next door."

Sam opened the screen door. Jen grinned as Sam walked in.

Then, Jen answered her mother. "Yeah, if the girl next door is half orangutan."

Sam wondered if her eyes actually bugged out.

"Jennifer!" Lila snapped, but she was facing the sink to pop ice cubes from a tray, not watching the mocking way Jen swung her arms.

First Pam had made a condescending remark about Jen's hair ties. Now Jen was actually mimicking Pam. They were acting like jealous little kids.

As the goofy grin faded from Jen's lips, Sam wondered if she was doing something to provoke this weirdness from her friends. She didn't think so, but she tried to appeal to Jen's sense of fairness.

"Pam *is* nearly six feet tall and she's an amazing basketball player," Sam said, "but middle school was hard for her. She was the tallest kid in the entire school, even taller than most of the teachers."

"Oh," Jen said. Then, at the sound of steps outside, she added, "There she is."

It was pretty quiet as the three of them sat at the little table on Jen's front porch, sipping lemonade and staring at the blue pottery plate of cookies.

Sam knew she wasn't favoring one of her friends over the other. She knew they'd like each other if each just gave the other a chance, but how could she make that happen?

Pam took a cookie from the plate and nibbled politely just as the iron gates slammed open. It couldn't possibly be Gram again. Not yet.

Ryan rode Sky Ranger down the road flanked with horses and cattle, but he didn't spare a glance for all the animals and flowers around him.

"Great! It's Ryan!" Pam said and she actually gave a little bounce of excitement in her wooden chair.

Perfect, Sam thought. *She* knew Pam was just pleased to see someone she recognized, but Jen didn't seem to be able to wrap her mind around such a simple idea. Not at all. In fact, if looks could kill, Pam wouldn't be chewing that chocolate chip cookie. She'd be choking on it.

Chapter Ten ❧

"They don't look very happy with each other," Sam said.

Something in her voice must have sliced through Jen's irritation, because she stopped glaring at Pam and took a good look at the horse and rider.

To the welcoming neighs of a dozen other horses, Ryan rode Sky Ranger toward the barn. Sky seemed to be walking on tiptoe. He mouthed his snaffle noisily and his ears twirled to catch every sound as if he were searching for a reason to act up.

Ryan gave the girls a curt wave, then looked down. Hands perfectly spaced on the single rein, he stayed focused on his horse.

"They've been out since the sun rose," Jen said

slowly, "but *that*" — Jen pointed as Sky's hindquarters swiveled to one side before he launched a kick — "isn't the action of a tired horse. And *that*," she said as Ryan slapped Sky with the flat of his hand, "says they're totally fed up with each other. Ryan's too good a horseman to let Sky get the better of him like that."

As one, all three girls stood, but Jen took the lead as they approached Ryan and his mount.

"Is it okay if I come along?" Pam asked.

"You might as well," Sam answered.

"There aren't many secrets on a ranch," Jen added.

Ryan's dark hair was ruffled and dusty. Judging by Sky's sweat-stiff coat, the gelding had definitely worked hard, but Jen was right. Something else was wrong.

For a single moment, Ryan grinned. He looked delighted to see Jen striding toward him with her usual energy, but then his face closed up again.

As if he were in the show ring, Ryan signaled his horse to back up. The Thoroughbred lashed his tail and kicked out with a single hind leg. When Ryan cued the gelding to move forward, he hopped and grunted.

"This horse doesn't know how to travel in a straight line," Ryan complained.

Jen tilted her head. As she studied Sky, one of her long white-blond braids hung past her shoulder and swung like a wildly decorated pendulum.

"He's known how to travel in a straight line since

the day he was born," Jen told Ryan. "If you can't communicate what you want from him, that's your fault."

Ryan's face turned crimson.

"I beg your pardon?" he snapped. Looking down from his seat atop the tall horse, he frowned at the girls as if they were lower life forms.

"Just think about it," Jen said gently. "And in the meantime, get down and let me try something."

Ryan kept staring at them, but apparently his lips could only hold that "Who do you think you are?" sneer for so long, because he gave a half smile as he jerked a dusty boot free of his stirrup iron and dismounted.

"He's all yours," Ryan said. "Hello Samantha and Pamela. Lovely to see you, and I do hope you're both enjoying this dressing-down Jen is giving me."

Sam made a noncommittal sound and Pam shrugged as Ryan tossed Sky's rein to Jen. She caught it, but her grab was stiff, not graceful.

"Are you really up to bronco busting?" Ryan asked as he touched her shoulder.

"I don't think there'll be any of that," Jen said. This time she was the one blushing. "Besides, if I mess up you can come rescue me." She led Sky a few steps and when the Thoroughbred looked back over his shoulder, Jen did, too. "Who knows, you might get knighted or something."

Ryan shook his head. As Jen led his horse away, he looked after her with something like admiration.

So did Pam. Then she turned to Sam, nodded wildly and made an "okay" sign with her fingers.

If standing up to Ryan was what it took to earn Jen acceptance from Pam, Sam guessed that was okay. But she hoped Jen wasn't in over her head.

Jen gave a small gasp and hunched forward for a second after she'd slung Sky's rein over the fence with a little too much force. Her ribs were still mending, no matter how tough she thought she was. Sam cringed as Jen stripped off the gelding's small saddle, then she sent silent thanks to Sky for lowering his head as Jen reached behind his ears to remove his bridle. Jen kept the rein looped around his neck.

At least she wasn't going to try riding him. That was a relief.

Ryan held his hands palms up and apart, frowning, as he looked questioningly at Sam. She shook her head.

"I have no idea what she's up to," Sam told him. And then, from the corner of her eye, she noticed Jed Kenworthy was watching his daughter, too.

Judging by his thumbs-in-pockets stance, Jed, who stood in the barn's shade, didn't know what was coming next, either.

Jen swung open the gate of Shy Boots's empty paddock, pulled the rein off, and turned Sky loose.

A sensible person, Sam thought, would have ducked away from the horse and let him work out his bad mood alone. Instead, when Sky began bucking and kicking at the clouds, Jen followed him inside and closed the gate behind her.

Her four-person audience pressed closer to the fence to watch.

At first, Jen only stood near the gate. That was scary enough for Sam.

Seeing Jen in a confined space with a dangerous animal was too much like the day she'd seen her best friend attacked by the Hereford bull.

"I don't like this," Sam told Ryan. "I don't like this one bit."

"Tell me she knows what she's doing," Pam demanded. "Please."

Before she answered, Sam glanced at Jed Kenworthy. Jen was still on thin ice with her father. Sam didn't want to do anything to make him unsure of her safety.

"She knows what she's doing," Sam insisted.

"But sometimes that ain't enough," Jed cut in.

Pam faced Sam with widened eyes. She waggled her brows and rolled her eyes in Jed's direction, as if to ask who this critical cowboy was, but Sam made a delaying gesture.

She'd have to tell Pam later. Right now, Jen needed quiet so she could concentrate on the agitated horse.

Sky's bucking slackened. He broke into a staccato trot. As he circled the paddock, his tail swished, then he squealed in fury and commenced bucking again.

"That's it," Jed said under his breath, as his

daughter's attention shifted. "Watch his hind end."

At Jed's satisfied tone, Ryan leaned his crossed arms against the fence. He studied the gelding so hard, his brows almost met in the center.

Sam felt a little sorry for Ryan as he tried to figure out Sky's misbehavior before anyone else. He'd been Sky's rider. He should know what was wrong.

Sky stopped, tail held high as an Arabian. Jen came closer and he fidgeted, as if he wanted to run, but he didn't. When she held her arms wide, then rushed toward him, he bolted, tail tucked for a second before he broke into another powerful, dusty round of bucking.

"I'm stumped," Sam told Jed. "He doesn't move like he's hurt."

At that, Ryan's head whipped toward her.

"I would never overwork a horse. Certainly not to the point of injury."

"I know. I didn't mean—" Sam answered, but then they all heard Jen talking baby talk.

"Sweetie, I'll help you," she said to Sky. She strolled closer to the horse with her arms down at her sides. "I'll get all those nasty stickers out of your tail so they don't hurt you anymore."

"Stickers?" Ryan asked in an undertone.

He only looked ashamed for a second, then his eyes lost focus and Sam guessed he was reviewing his day, trying to recall when and where they'd encountered stickers.

"There was a sort of bramble hedge," Ryan mused, "with dried-up blackberries. A covey of quail burst out from under it. But it was some little distance off."

Ryan was still shaking his head when Jed turned to him.

"Musta somehow stuck to the underside of his tail," Jed said, "and since it looks to me as if she's determined to get 'em off—I'll tell you, son, I'd be obliged if you'd go in and help her."

"At once," Ryan said.

Was Ryan responding to Jed's trust, his calm use of the word *son*, or did Ryan just want to help Jen before she needed the rescue she'd joked about? Sam didn't know, but with more speed and grace than she would have expected, Ryan hopped the fence. And for a guy who'd just been shown up by his girlfriend, Ryan looked pretty happy.

Sam watched as his eyes met Jen's and held them for a minute.

"Feeling all right, are you?"

"I feel great," Jen said.

While they soothed Sky with voices and firm pats and plucked the stickers from his tail, Pam shook her head.

"Your friend's amazing," Pam said.

"Jen really knows horses," Sam agreed.

"Yeah, but it's more than that." Pam pulled Sam close enough to hear her whisper, "She did what she knew how to do, even though it made her boyfriend mad and her dad nuts."

"Yeah," Sam agreed. "That's sort of how cowgirls are."

"I wish I could be like that. I hate taking a chance on falling flat on my face," Pam said in a normal tone. "But she just charged in and appointed herself the boss." Pam rolled her eyes toward Sam. "In the nicest possible way, of course."

"Of course," Sam said.

Once Ryan and Jen had finished, Jen's hands were shaking and she leaned against the fence. But just for a second. When she saw her dad watching, Jen pushed off from the fence, squared her shoulders, and lifted her chin.

"Hi, Dad," she said, sounding casual as she walked back toward the gate.

Ryan rushed ahead to open it for her, then bowed her through.

"Don't you be 'hi, Dad-ing' me all innocent like," Jed told her. "I saw the whole danged thing."

A series of expressions crossed Jen's face. First she was appalled, then defiant, and finally resigned. Then, looking a little bit proud, she took off her glasses, turned the hem of her lime green T-shirt inside out to polish her lenses, and asked, "What'd you think?"

"Humph. Don't matter what I think. All I know's if your doctor's willin', I'm sending you back to school on Monday, so you don't give me a heart attack."

With that, Jed stalked toward the foreman's house. He moved fast and Sam couldn't help thinking he wanted to get inside before Jen's cowgirl yell split the afternoon.

But he didn't make it.

Once her excitement settled into satisfaction, Jen talked with the other girls as Ryan groomed Sky Ranger near the barn.

"Sam, I've got to have your honest opinion," Jen insisted.

"I think you should go inside and take a nap," Sam said.

"Not about that," Jen said. "I want to give Ryan some more advice about Sky and I don't know whether this is a great time or a terrible one to do that."

"How would I know?" Sam asked. She stared toward the barn.

As sweetly as a pet dog shaking hands, Sky lifted a hoof to be cleaned.

"He said there was no sign of Hotspot and he didn't see a single mustang. I think he should switch horses, but I'm not sure he'd welcome my advice, since I just kind of—"

"Beat him at his own game?" Sam interrupted. After all, the one thing Ryan excelled at was horsemanship.

"I guess," Jen said moodily. Then, slowly, she

faced Pam, but she had to look up past the tall girl's black-and-white jersey to do it. "What do you think?"

"Me?" Pam put both hands on her chest. "I think you were amazing with both of them—Ryan and the horse," Pam said without a trace of embarrassment.

Jen gave a surprised laugh. "A girl of rare taste and judgment," she joked. "You know how to pick friends, Sam."

"Yes, I do," she agreed.

"But," Pam took the conversation back just as skillfully as she'd steal a basketball, "I've been on a lot of coed teams with guys, and I am blown away at how nice he's being about you showing him up."

Ryan had turned Sky out into Gold Dust Ranch's saddle horse pen and he was coming back their way.

"Me too," Sam said. "Especially for—" She'd been about to say, *Especially for a Slocum.* "A guy."

"But if I don't say anything now, he'll probably ride Sky out again tomorrow morning," Jen said.

"He needs to ride a horse that's a little less intense," Sam said. "I almost never see mustangs on any horse except Ace."

"Exactly," Jen said. "I've got to say something."

"I'll back you up," Sam said. "I mean, Jake and I did what he's trying to do."

Sam still didn't think this was the right time to tell Ryan he was doing something else wrong, but Jen looked determined.

"Okay," Pam said, surrendering, "but if he tries to

compliment you on handling his horse, pretend you lucked out."

"I will *not,*" Jen said. "I knew from the moment he rode in here—"

"I'm just saying," Pam told her, then nodded toward Ryan.

He looked different, more willful than he had when wearing Jed's praise.

"What are you three plotting?" he asked suspiciously.

"Well," Jen said with a relieved sigh. "If you really want to know—"

"Wait." Ryan jabbed his palm toward her, as if it could halt her words. "I don't."

"Ryan," Jen stretched his name out teasingly.

"Not if it's advice about Hotspot," Ryan insisted. He shook his dark hair away from eyes that looked angry.

Apparently Jen didn't notice, because she said, "Ryan, don't be silly."

"Excuse me," Pam said. She held up an index finger, and stepped away from the others. "I left my lemonade over on the porch, in the shade. I think I'll go keep it company."

Then, as Pam passed by Sam, she added, "Think that's far enough away that I won't be struck by any flying chunks of shattered ego?"

Chapter Eleven ও৵

Sam considered following Pam to the front porch. She could sit in the shade and sip lemonade. That would be more fun than standing here, watching Jen and Ryan have an argument that wouldn't end well. But would Jen feel abandoned?

Probably not, but loyalty kept Sam standing by Jen's side just the same.

"You need to ride a horse Hotspot can see as a buddy," Jen said. "Sky is a competitor. She must feel hunted when he's out there."

Ryan's expressionless face didn't move. He could tolerate her advice, it seemed, waiting for her to stop talking.

"He's a great horse," Sam said, in case Ryan took

Jen's words as criticism of Sky Ranger. "But he's kind of dominant. Jake and I used Chip instead of Witch, his bossy mare, when we were riding after that paint filly."

Ryan squinted toward the pasture, ignoring her.

"Ryan, it's the same thing," Sam insisted.

"You two can't stand anyone to be more expert on horses than you are. I understand that," Ryan said. "And Jen, I don't blame you for being nervous about Sky after he threw you in the Superbowl of Horsemanship."

"I don't hold grudges against horses." Jen might have been stating a personal rule. Her tone said she didn't blame Sky for his reaction to the once-in-a-life-time appearance of stampeding buffalo.

"And you, Samantha," Ryan continued, "cannot accept that the Western way is not the only way to do things. That's rather ironic since you're a relative newcomer to this culture yourself."

"Except that she was born here," Jen pointed out.

"True, but when I was telling Pamela about you wearing leather chaps and a fancy fringed shirt for the talent show, she said this lifestyle was quite a switch for you. She claims you loved visiting museums and attending the symphony in San Francisco."

"So?" Sam demanded.

Ryan didn't answer. He didn't try to explain why she shouldn't like ranch life as well as city attractions.

Sam tried to make an allowance for Ryan. He probably felt like they'd ganged up on him. And Pam was right. Their timing was bad. He'd already been a gracious loser once today.

Still, he'd managed to make Jen feel jealous because he'd been chatting with Pam, and Sam feel sad because Pam was talking behind her back.

Except, Sam realized, Pam hadn't said anything bad. It was Ryan who'd put a sarcastic spin on Pam's San Francisco memories.

"Fine," she said, sounding weary. "But what does any of this have to do with Hotspot?"

"Just this," Ryan said. "I know what I'm doing."

"Okay," Jen said. "But could you take these three things into consideration? Hotspot is stable born and bred. The open range has always made her a little skittish. This is the second time she's run loose with horses that are instantly responsive to sounds and smells."

"That's right," Sam said. "Diablo stole her before, so she's developed some wild instincts."

As Sam remembered Diablo, she stared at his son. What had the hammerhead stallion contributed to Shy Boots? So far, the little Appaloosa looked and acted just like his mother.

"I saw quite a flurry of hoofprints near Snake's Head Peak and I happened to talk with Caleb," Ryan said without acknowledging Jen's information.

"Great," Sam said, bracing for disaster.

Caleb Sawyer was a troublemaker. Yes, he was old and hard of hearing. Yes, he had an aged dog he loved and he still held a grudging admiration for Sam's mother, but the former mustanger didn't deserve much sympathy.

Caleb Sawyer had tutored Linc Slocum in cruel and violent horse capture techniques. That's why the Phantom's neck was scarred. If Caleb Sawyer had given Ryan the same sort of advice, she'd march right into the Kenworthys' kitchen, pick up the phone, and call Sheriff Ballard.

Sam glanced over to see that Jen's arms were crossed, too.

"Caleb suggested using Shy Boots as—"

His voice broke off, but Sam knew what he'd been about to say.

"Bait?" Sam asked. She glanced over to see Shy Boots pick a shady spot for a nap. He lowered himself, folded his long legs, and closed his eyes.

He looked almost peaceful and all the emotion Sam had tried to tamp down exploded. "Using him for bait is a terrible idea! When you talked me into leaving him in the canyon, nothing ate him, but what makes you think you'll be that lucky twice?"

"I don't have to listen to this," Ryan said. His hand covered an aristocratic yawn, but then he looked at Jen. His expression changed when he saw she looked almost ready to cry.

"It's been over a month," Jen said. "What if he and Hotspot don't—"

"They'll recognize each other, Jennifer," Ryan assured her.

"Maybe," Jen said.

Her friend's weariness spurred Sam on.

"What if they do recognize each other, but Hotspot still doesn't come to him? Look how peaceful he is," Sam said, pointing. "Do you want to break his heart all over again?"

"That's such rubbish," Ryan said. "He's a horse, not a human."

A sudden whirlwind chased through the ranch yard, blowing dust that pecked at Sam's cheeks. Trying not to breathe in, she ducked away from it. The others did the same, and Sam used the moment to try to get a grip on her feelings.

Attacking Ryan obviously wasn't working, so she tried a different approach.

"Okay, I'll admit you know Hotspot better than I do," Sam said. After Ryan's nod, she went on. "Let's say everything goes like you think it will. From curiosity or memory or whatever, Hotspot comes to Boots. She's standing next to him out on the range somewhere. What do you do next?"

"I'd rope her. I may not be skilled with a lariat, but I believe I could rope her and lead her home."

Jen held her hands protectively over her rib as she coughed from the dust, then asked, "And if she sees you coming?"

"I'll chase her down and then rope her."

Ryan's plan would never work. Sam had practiced for long, frustrating hours, and she was still a barely passable roper. Her loops fell short or flew wide more often than they snared even a stationary target like a fencepost. Ryan could be a natural-born roper, and he'd still need hours of practice to rope a running horse from the saddle of the horse chasing her.

And that wasn't all. Hotspot was a sweet, gentle young mare. Through her pregnancy and Shy Boots's birth, she'd trusted Ryan. After she'd been run to exhaustion and choked into submission with his beginner's rope skills, how would she feel about him?

"You know Hotspot's temperament. How will she tolerate that aggressive stuff?" Sam asked.

It happened so quickly, Sam almost missed it. Ryan's forehead crinkled and his mouth drooped at the corners. He looked like a timid little boy, before his expression turned bland and he shrugged.

"She'll get over it."

Then Ryan left her and Jen, the corrals, and the barn. Without a wave or a good-bye, he walked back to his father's pillared mansion.

Pam must have watched him leave. Right away, she came striding from the porch and stopped beside Sam.

"So how'd it go?" she asked.

"Not so good," Sam said, but Jen corrected her.

"Terrible."

Pam sighed, but she didn't say "I told you so."

Sam watched her two friends look at each other in a considering way. She craved a peek into their minds. What were they thinking?

She didn't ask. Instead, when she heard Ryan

slam the mansion's heavy front door, she thought of Mrs. Coley, who lived in that grand house with three rich but unhappy people.

Mostly, she was talking to Jen when she said, "Mrs. Coley thinks this is all about Ryan proving himself to his dad."

"Mrs. Coley's their housekeeper," Jen told Pam, "and I guess she's right. But no matter what Ryan does, it's not going to work."

"I don't know," Sam said. "If he catches Hotspot and brings her home, I think Linc would be totally impressed. After all, that's the kind of Western . . ." Sam searched for a word. "*Test* that Linc's been trying to pass since he got here. It's why he wanted to capture the Phantom."

"Exactly," Jen said. "He's failed every time, but Ryan will probably succeed."

"I haven't met his father—" Pam began.

"Oh, you're in for a treat," Sam said sarcastically.

"—but you can't believe how many guys are in sports to please their dads. Next time you're at a basketball or baseball game, watch when some guy makes a great play. You'd be surprised how many of them—before they even smile—glance up into the stands to make sure their dads are happy."

"I need to think about that," Jen said, and her eyes lost focus for a moment.

While her friend was lost in thought, Sam decided Jen could worry about Ryan, but Sam was more concerned for Shy Boots.

Right now, before the Phantom moved his herd to his secret valley for the winter, Ryan needed to make his move.

The Phantom's herd had slipped away from BLM's helicopters many times, and they might do it again. If Hotspot fled with them, Shy Boots would be without her until next year. Kitty might seem like a fine stand-in mother to the humans, but what if Shy Boots didn't agree? Should they risk "failure to thrive" and a possible ulcer if Hotspot might cure him?

"What do you think about using Mocha?" Sam asked suddenly.

"Mocha? Like the espresso drink?" Pam asked, looking baffled. "For what?"

"Not the drink," Jen said, smiling. Then she pointed to a far pasture. "The horse."

Mocha was the show-quality Morgan that belonged to Rachel. The mare was even-tempered, strong, and levelheaded. As far as Sam knew, Rachel had never ridden her. She'd actually convinced her father to buy the expensive horse because they had the same coffee-brown hair.

"Mocha would be perfect for going after Hotspot," Jen agreed. "And she could use the work." Jen glanced toward the mansion. Lights glowed from its upstairs windows, though the downstairs stood dark. "I'll mention Mocha to Ryan."

"I'm telling you," Pam put in. "You have to make him think he came up with the idea."

"That's totally sexist," Sam pointed out.

"True, but based on the other competitive guys I know, it's the only way," Pam said.

"He *is* supercompetitive," Jen conceded.

A fall breeze had rushed in after the dusty whirlwind. Sam smelled dry leaves and rabbit brush. She held back the hair blowing over her eyes and saw Jen shiver.

Northern Nevada could change from summer to autumn in a single day.

From hot to cold, just like some people. Just like Ryan. Sam wished he'd either grow up or quit making her friend as confused as he was.

But Jen's thoughts had turned back to horses, too.

"One good thing about the nights getting colder," Jen said, "is since horses have the best memories in the world, Hotspot might remember her cozy stall and decide it's time to come in from the wild."

"Maybe," Sam said, but her spirits were lower than they'd been all day.

They'd stood quiet for a minute, watching the day end around them, when a coyote's howl rose from the range.

Pam jumped. Her mouth and eyes rounded with alarm and her arms jerked as if someone had shouted "Hands up!"

"It's just a—" Jen and Sam said together.

"A coyote. I know," Pam said, rubbing the goose bumps from her bare arms. "And I am such a city mouse, they terrify me."

All three girls laughed.

A city mouse, Sam thought, smiling.

She couldn't remember the details of that fable about the country mouse and the city mouse, but she thought the rodent cousins learned they each had the skills to match their surroundings.

Sam looked at her two friends. Cowgirl Jen knew almost everything there was to know about horses. As a San Francisco athlete, Pam knew what made competitive guys like Ryan tick.

If those two teamed up, Ryan Slocum might realize he couldn't take any shortcuts. He had to remind Hotspot she still loved him. Then he could bring her home to her baby.

The next day at school Sam was called down to the office.

On a bench in front of the counselors' offices sat Pam. She jumped to her feet the minute she spotted Sam.

"I'm so glad to see you," Pam muttered as they walked through the quiet halls back to Sam's English class. "Am I dressed okay?"

"Sure," Sam said, because it wasn't Pam's clothes she'd noticed.

As far as Sam was concerned, jeans and a polo shirt always looked about right, but Pam was carrying a basketball. Actually, carrying wasn't exactly the right word. She was palming it, walking along holding it as if her long fingers had suction cups on the tips.

"You look great," Sam added.

"But you're wondering why I brought my basketball." Pam took a deep breath. "I don't know. Call it a security blanket, I guess. I take it everywhere, except restaurants. Mom makes me leave it in the truck."

"That's why you won the city championship. You love basketball and it loves you," Sam said.

"You were really good, too," Pam reminded her.

"*Were*, is sort of the point," Sam said. "I doubt I could even hit the rim anymore."

"Hey, I know," Pam said. "Do they have open gym here during lunchtime? I'd love to throw the ball around with you a little bit."

"Yeah, like that thought just popped into your brain this very instant," Sam teased.

"Maybe it crossed my mind before," Pam said. She danced a few steps down the corridor, dribbling the ball, then pivoted and shot it right at Sam's hands.

Sam caught it.

"I don't know," Sam said as she launched the ball back at Pam.

But even as she uttered the words, she knew she'd give in. It sounded like fun.

It was, and any qualms Sam had about people thinking she looked lame evaporated when she discovered no one was watching her. All eyes tracked Pam.

In fact, Pam almost made Sam late to Journalism

because the coach supervising open gym wouldn't let Pam go.

Sam had stood in the gym doorway, shifting from foot to foot as the first bell rang and Pam stood spinning the ball on one finger until it wobbled and she caught it with her other hand, then doing it again and again while the coach kept talking.

Finally, with just seconds to go, Pam sprinted toward Sam.

"He wouldn't let me leave," Pam gasped. "He thought I was lying to him about being from out of town. He thought I was just shy or something. I finally had to show him my visitor's pass."

They barely made it to Journalism. As Sam worked on her assignment, Pam pulled a desk up beside her. Together, they schemed about how to help Ryan catch Hotspot.

"You should know how it's done," Pam whispered. "Since you get your stallion to come to you and he's totally wild."

Sam was nodding before Pam finished. She'd been thinking about that subject half the night.

"He can't chase her, trap her, or tear her away from her herd," Sam said. "He has to make Hotspot want to come to him."

The sudden rasp of Mr. Blair clearing his throat made Sam freeze. She tightened her grip on her pencil, wiggled the eraser end, and frowned as if she were perplexed over her work.

When she sneaked a glance at her teacher, though, Sam could see he wasn't fooled. Mr. Blair pointed down at the paperwork on his desk, then returned to reading it as if he expected her to do the same.

"He's not going to kick me out, is he?" Pam asked.

"No," Sam said. "He won't cut me any slack on my deadline, but he knows I'll do what I have to do to get it in."

By the time class ended and Sam and Pam were walking toward the school parking lot, Sam had warned Pam about the ride to Gold Dust Ranch.

"We'll be sharing that baby-blue Mercedes," Sam said, pointing at the car, "with Ryan's evil twin, Rachel."

Pam was braced and ready to be either scorned or ignored by the rich girl, but then a weird thing happened. Rachel was nicer to Pam than Sam had ever seen her be to another girl. She was so nice, Sam could hardly believe this person in the front seat beside Mrs. Coley was really Rachel.

She smelled like Rachel, wearing a musky perfume that filled the car. She sounded like Rachel, her musical voice lilting with an American accent on the high notes and British on the low ones. She certainly looked like Rachel, totally chic in black slacks and an inappropriate-for-school silver top that would have looked like layers of fraying duct tape on anyone else.

But this person didn't act like Rachel. When Pam leaned forward to ask about the unusual blouse, she didn't sigh condescendingly.

"This?" Rachel said, pulling a piece of the fabric clear of her seat belt and looking down at it as if she'd forgotten what she'd put on that morning. "I'm glad you like it. I wasn't sure if maybe it was a little too trendy, but I got it in a little shop somewhere this summer."

Too trendy? Got it "somewhere"? The Rachel Sam knew would have rattled off the address of a charming little boutique that most mortals didn't know existed, on Rue de whatever in Paris.

I don't get it, Sam thought.

And now Rachel was twisting in her seat to ask Pam about San Francisco's weather and music scene, about her school and classes, her travel with her basketball team, and even how she'd met Sam.

Guilt was making Sam regret what she'd told Pam, until Sam looked up and caught the reflection of Mrs. Coley's eyes in the rearview mirror. The housekeeper was astonished as well.

What is she playing at? Sam wondered, but she sat back in her seat to wait.

The real Rachel didn't show up until the Mercedes passed Jake, once more jogging at the roadside. Today, he wore Darton High's green-and-gold uniform and ran toward the front of a group of cross-country team members. Sam had wanted to introduce Pam to Jake, but she hadn't spotted him in the halls even once.

"I think he's letting his hair grow out again," Sam

commented as they passed. She hadn't meant to say it. The words just slipped out.

"Which one?" Pam asked, turning to stare out the car's back window.

Sam was pointing at Jake when Rachel said, "The one with the mahogany skin and ebony hair. Jake."

Sam hadn't realized Rachel knew words like *mahogany* and *ebony*, but her mocking pronunciation of "Jake" was familiar.

Pam's eyebrows quirked up and she looked at Sam. Rachel's implication was pretty easy to understand.

"He's not my boyfriend," Sam said flatly.

"Oh, right," Rachel sneered.

"We're just friends."

Rachel leaned her head so close to Pam's, it looked like she was going to tell her a secret. But she didn't whisper.

Sam had no trouble hearing Rachel say, "You know what *that* means."

"Probably that they're just friends," Pam answered. Until now, she'd seemed as charmed by Rachel as she'd been—at first—by Ryan. Now, Pam scooted closer to Sam.

Rachel looked unsettled, but she wasn't finished.

"When we get back to the house, I hope you'll come in for a little tour."

Sam turned with such surprise, her shoulder bumped Pam's. She'd never been past the front door of the Slocums' mansion.

"Go ahead," Sam told Pam.

"No, that's okay," Pam said, giving Sam a small jab with her elbow.

"But Ryan said he thought you'd like a break from, you know, Sam and Jennifer's horse stuff."

"I'm actually kind of enjoying the horse stuff. I've ridden a little bit, but I'm not good at it, and today . . ." Pam drew the last word out suspensefully as she folded her hands atop her basketball. For the first time, Rachel gave it a sidelong glance, as if she'd been trying all this time to ignore it, sitting round and orange on Pam's lap, "I promised Sam that if she played basketball with me, I'd go riding with her."

That was news to Sam, but she didn't leave Pam any room to wriggle away from the statement.

"Yep, and I'm holding her to her promise," Sam said. "No matter what."

Giving a theatrical sigh, Rachel gazed out the car window.

"I'm surrounded by people who adore horses, and I can't understand why. They're dumb, and dirty, and riding them increases even the most coordinated person's opportunities for looking clumsy and inept."

"I hope not," Pam began, but then she leaned forward. "But, hmm, I see what you mean."

It took Sam a few seconds to see past Pam and a few seconds more to make out the bulbous form of Linc Slocum clinging to the neck of a beautiful palomino.

Chapter Twelve ❦

Sam had heard Pepper refer to people who "rode like a sack of potatoes," but she'd just figured that since Pepper was from Idaho, it was some regional saying.

But watching Linc Slocum try to keep up with Ryan, who rode ahead of him on Sky Ranger, Sam understood the words for the first time.

Even though a glare of silver saddle, spurs, and headstall surrounded him, Linc hadn't been able to buy horsemanship. His elbows flapped and he leaned back against his reins as he stood in the tapaderoed stirrups. Shaped like upside-down teardrops and coated with silver, they didn't hide his cruel spurs.

Sam was glad Jen wasn't here to see poor Champ.

Golden Champagne was one of the Kenworthy palominos. Part of their Fire and Ice breeding program, he had the sunshine coat, snowy mane, and intelligence the Kenworthys had worked so hard to create in their horses.

But if Champ hadn't yet been ruined by Linc's riding, he soon would be. How could the gelding know what to do? Linc's spurs forced Champ forward, but his ham-fisted grip on the reins yanked the bit into the hinge of the palomino's jaw, commanding him to stop.

Throw him, Sam thought. *Leave him to walk home in those high-heeled boots.*

But Champ didn't heed Sam's silent urging. He followed instincts that told him to ignore the conflicting orders from his rider and gallop after Sky Ranger, toward home.

Mrs. Coley slowed the car, letting the horses and riders go on ahead.

By the time they passed through the electronic gates of Gold Dust Ranch, Sam could see that Ryan and his father were standing together, arguing.

It looked like Ryan was stripping the tack from Sky Ranger, but Linc was too busy yelling to do the same for Champ. From inside the car, Sam couldn't hear Linc, but she saw the pumping of his arms and the way his head slung from side to side as he hurled out angry words.

Nearby, Champ wandered head down, reins trailing from his bit, making a careful escape.

Mrs. Coley braked in front of the foreman's house to let Pam and Sam out as far from the argument as possible.

"See you later," Sam said to Rachel as they climbed out of the car.

"It was nice meeting you," Pam added, leaning down to look back inside.

Was Rachel embarrassed by the argument between her father and brother? Or annoyed by Pam's refusal to fall under her spell?

Sam only knew that Rachel sat with her spine pressed against the back of her seat and didn't say a word.

As they headed toward Jen's porch, Sam and Pam realized they were almost close enough to eavesdrop on the Slocums' argument. So they did.

"What's a black baldy?" Pam asked, her face twisted in confusion.

"I'll tell you later," Sam said. "But it sounds like they're arguing about which beef cattle would be most profitable for the ranch and—" Sam paused a second, trying to listen. "Ryan knows what he's talking about. Linc is just repeating stuff he's heard."

"Another wild goose chase!" Linc bellowed.

"That was easy enough to understand," Pam whispered.

They both listened intently, but it was harder to make out Ryan's words because he didn't shout like his father.

Once, Sam was pretty sure she heard Ryan snarl, "I hope you're satisfied," but she had no idea what he was talking about.

Then Linc lowered his voice. It was still loud, but Sam could tell he was trying to sound logical as he made one more attempt at convincing Ryan to do things his way.

"Look, there's dozens of cowboys around here who wouldn't balk at taking a few hundred dollars to run her down and drag her back here."

Ryan's head snapped back as if he'd been slapped, as if his father's calm suggestion hit harder than his shouting.

"You think I want to buy my way out of this?" Ryan's voice rose in disbelief. "Well, I'm not like you!"

Linc twisted the top half of his body away from Ryan. He seemed stalled there for a second, or maybe he was hoping Ryan would take back the hurtful words, but then the rest of his body turned and he made his way toward his shiny Cadillac.

Tottering on his high-heeled boots, he shouted something about BLM over his shoulder, then yelled, "So take the rest of the week off!"

Ryan stood watching as Linc heaved himself into the Cadillac, gunned the engine so loudly that horses bolted in every pasture, then drove out of the ranch yard, gravel spitting from his tires.

Pam released a loud gust of breath. "Don't introduce me to him, okay?"

"Don't worry," Sam said.

"Hey," Jen said as she came out onto the porch. "That was quite the performance, wasn't it? Imagine living in the same house with that guy?"

Sam shook her head. She couldn't understand how Jen lived on the same *ranch* with Linc Slocum.

If Linc hadn't respected Jed Kenworthy's ranching skills, if he hadn't been smart enough to know Jed was the only thing keeping the Gold Dust in business, things would have been much worse.

"I wonder what my dad's saying to Ryan?" Jen mused, and they looked to see Jed standing near the younger Slocum.

They were having a serious talk, cowboy-style. Jed was looking down, kicking at the dirt, not making eye contact, but staying close.

"If Ryan has to pick someone to try to impress, he should pick your dad," Sam told Jen.

Maybe Jed Kenworthy was kind of old-fashioned and he didn't value mustangs as much as she did, but he knew you got important things by working for them, not buying them.

"Sam, that was so nice." Jen's voice was incredulous.

Blushing, Sam shrugged.

"Yeah, Sam," Pam said, holding her basketball in one hand and giving Sam a gentle punch with the other. "How come you never say anything like that about my mom?"

"But your mom's great. I—" Sam stopped when

Pam started laughing. "I think you should be quiet."

"Fine, then let's go see what they're talking about," Pam said.

"I'll go with you, but I'll be leaving for a doctor's appointment," Jen said. "I only have a few minutes."

By the time they reached Ryan, Jed had snagged Champ's reins.

"C'mon," Jed said to the horse.

His voice was gentle, but when he used the back of his hand to wipe bloody foam from the gelding's lips, then checked Champ's hot chest, anger suffused Jed's face. He'd bred this horse, watched him be foaled, and raised him. Seeing Champ treated like an unfeeling object must be making him furious.

"At least he doesn't do it much," Ryan said. "Ride, I mean."

"No," Jed agreed. "Like you said, he's losin' interest."

Ryan forked his fingers through the front of his hair. He looked frustrated but thoughtful. "I don't know what that means for the rest of us."

"Doesn't do to dwell on it," Jed said. "About your mare, though? I think you're on the right track."

Ryan hesitated, staring toward the electronic gate after his father. He swallowed audibly and Sam wondered if that meant he was giving up, for now at least, on trying to please his father.

"Bring her in without all that helicopter hoopla," Jed suggested.

"I will," Ryan said, then he watched without

blinking as Jed pulled the silver-mounted bridle from Champ's head. With a groan, the palomino rubbed his forelock against Jed's chest.

Sam didn't realize they were all watching the horse thank the man until Champ blew through his lips and the foreman looked away.

Then they all followed Jed's eyes. He looked pointedly at Sky Ranger.

Turned out in the corral and stripped of tack, Sky still had a sweaty patch from his saddle.

Without saying anything, Ryan moved toward the horse, letting Jed know he planned to do better than his father.

As Sam and Pam walked Jen toward her mother, they revised their strategy.

"I think we should just leave him alone," Jen said.

"Me too," Sam agreed. "Did you hear him tell Linc he wasn't like him?"

"Wasn't that great?" Jen said. She bit her lip and looked toward Pam. "Let's just let him think about it." Then, when Pam didn't offer any sign of agreement, Jen said, "Don't you think that's the right thing to do? Just let him think it over?"

"Probably," Pam said, nodding. "But I was just remembering what my coach on my old coed team told me when one of the guys was driving me crazy."

"What's that?" Sam asked. She could see the sparkle in Pam's eyes that signaled a joke.

"He said, 'Pamster . . .' That's what they called

me, 'cause I was quick as a hamster—"

"Go on!" Sam pleaded.

"Okay. 'Pamster,' he said, 'don't spend too much time trying to figure out what guys are thinking; they don't do it very often.'"

Gram arrived just minutes after Lila and Jen left for the doctor's office. As they drove, Sam asked Gram to take them home to River Bend instead of driving out to Pam's camp at Lost Canyon.

"We're going for a ride," Sam said.

"Oh, it's so nice that you ride, Pam," Gram said.

"That remains to be seen," Pam said, and Sam heard the echo of Dr. Mora in her words. "I've done it, but I'm definitely not experienced."

Sam and Gram discussed which horse Pam should ride. Strawberry was gentle, but liked her own way; Ace liked to pull tricks on unwary riders; and Jeepers-Creepers had been known to crow-hop if he didn't like the look of his own shadow.

"Hey, I know," Pam said. "Why don't we just drive?"

"We don't keep a mean horse on the ranch," Gram assured her.

"And a promise is a promise," Sam said.

"Oh, but wait," Pam said, holding up an index finger as if she'd found a way out. "What will I do with my basketball? I can't carry it on a horse."

"We'll think of something, dear," Gram said. "If

nothing else, we could put it in one of those hay nets and tie it in place on your saddle. Now, I hope you can stay for dinner. We're having a front-porch picnic—cold fried chicken, potato salad, and—"

"Don't tell me any more," Pam said, covering her ears. "Mom made me promise to come back to camp."

"Maybe tomorrow," Gram said. "You could even spend the night, if you like."

"Yeah!" Sam and Pam chorused, and all the way back to the ranch, they made plans for a Friday night sleepover.

Tank, Nike, and Blue Wings were gone from the saddle pasture, but that still left lots of horses to choose from.

Pam fell in love with Penny, Brynna's mare, at first sight.

"That's it. I've decided," she said when Penny stood at the fence nuzzling her hand.

But then Sam explained the mare's blindness. "And it's not that I think Brynna would mind if you rode her," Sam said. "It's just that Penny's minus one of her senses. She's pretty dependent on her rider for direction."

"Whoa," Pam said to Sam. "She's not for me, then. I've been trying to count, and I think I've only been on a horse five times. And none of those were out in the, you know, wide open. So, you pick. Give me the tamest horse you've got."

"Okay," Sam said slowly.

At last Sam decided on Popcorn. Although the albino gelding had once been wild, he worked well with the HARP girls and his tall, free-moving gait fit Pam's.

Sam saddled up for both of them and Pam proved to be more comfortable riding Popcorn than she'd thought.

"There's only one thing I'm worried about," Pam said as they crossed the bridge over the La Charla River. "What if we ride into the middle of a stampede of wild horses? Is he going to buck me off?"

"That's not going to happen," Sam assured her. "If wild horses hear us coming, they'll be gone."

"But is Popcorn going to take off with them?"

"I don't think so," Sam said. "After all, I'm riding a mustang, too, and if I thought there was anything to worry about—"

"You don't *think so*?" Pam said.

"Do you want to ride back to the ranch and get Gram to drive us after all?" Sam asked.

For one fraction of a second, she wanted Pam to say yes.

Since Popcorn had lived in captivity, he'd had lots of kind care and skilled handling. He wasn't likely to take off after wild ones as they ran, but she didn't want to be responsible for Pam's safety if that did happen.

"Never mind. I'll be fine," Pam said. "Besides, you were brave enough to play basketball with me, so I guess it's my turn to prove I have some guts."

Chapter Thirteen ❧

Mustangs rarely drank at the lake at War Drum Flats unless it was dawn or dusk. Although the summer sun wouldn't drop below the horizon for at least two more hours, clouds had crowded in front of the sun, dropping the late afternoon temperature, bringing a wild herd down from the foothills.

The girls had been riding along, talking about the Chinese language class Pam would be taking in school. Her mom had urged her to sign up for it because of a research trip Dr. Mora had planned, to study stories of China's spotted Heavenly Horses.

Pam and Popcorn got along fine until they followed Sam and Ace downhill from the highway. Popcorn snorted, pulled to the right, and resisted

Pam's clucking encouragement as they headed toward the shallow lake.

"Sam, what should I do?"

"He'll be okay," Sam said, but then she looked away from Popcorn to the territory ahead and saw what the albino gelding did.

The Phantom's herd drank in the shallows of the lake, and the big honey-colored mare had spotted them.

Sam didn't take her eyes from the wild horses, even when Pam gasped behind her.

"If we stay really still, maybe they won't see us," Pam said, halting her horse. She leaned low on Popcorn's neck as if she could hide.

"Too late," Sam said. "The lead mare already sees us."

"The big gold one?" Pam asked. "Are you sure?"

"Pretty sure," Sam said.

Even though the lead mare's head was down and she still appeared to be drinking, the mare looked tense. She could bolt and alarm the rest of the herd at any second.

Ace felt himself being watched. He took a step backward. Popcorn did the same. They both recognized the mare's authority.

"I thought the stallion was the boss," Pam said quietly.

"He's the protector," Sam whispered, "but the lead mare decides where they eat and drink, and she disciplines the colts so that they know how to act."

Pam's breath caught as another horse jostled the lead mare.

"That's Ryan's horse, right? She looks just like her baby."

"That's Hotspot," Sam agreed, "and she'd better quit crowding the lead mare."

The honey-colored mare flattened her ears into her flaxen mane and swung her head toward Hotspot.

The Appaloosa ignored the warning and lowered her cocoa-brown muzzle right where the lead mare's had been. At once, the lead mare's lips tightened, showing her teeth, and she lunged.

Hotspot splashed back a step, shaking her mane.

"Is she going to bite her?" Pam asked.

"She will if she doesn't back off," Sam said. "See how the others are keeping their distance from the lead mare? At least a couple yards? I guess Hotspot never learned herd manners."

"But she was trying to be friends," Pam protested.

"I know, but the mare's on guard. It's sort of like . . ." Sam searched her mind for an example. "I don't know, like, if your teacher was grading papers and you ran up and gave her a hug."

The lead mare's ears stayed flat and her eyes narrowed, but Hotspot didn't move off. With a dripping muzzle, she watched Sam and Pam.

She just didn't have wild instincts, Sam thought. Instead of being wary or at least paying attention to the lead mare's tension, Hotspot radiated curiosity as she flicked her ears toward the riders. Raising her head for a better view, she bumped the lead mare and didn't seem to notice when the gold horse turned away and raised one of her hind legs.

"She's going to get kicked," Sam said, but just then Hotspot spotted the lead mare's lashing flaxen tail. "She's still not taking the hint."

Instead of showing her respect by getting out of the lead mare's space, Hotspot snorted and her own ears flicked flat.

"Uh-oh," Pam gasped as the lead mare struck out, kicking the Appaloosa.

Hotspot lunged with teeth exposed, but the lead mare didn't let her bite. Instead, she used both hind hooves to kick out at the younger mare.

Hotspot squealed, swapped ends, and launched a double-hooved kick at the lead mare. It struck with a meaty thump.

"No," Sam moaned. "Wild horses don't just attack each other. Mostly they just warn and threaten. They know a real fight could hurt a herd member and she could fall behind and get eaten. Even stallions don't—"

Shocked by Hotspot's violence, the lead mare waited a few disbelieving seconds before returning the kick, and Hotspot was able to sidestep it. But the lead mare kept backing, threshing hooves turning the water white. Hotspot bolted for the shore.

Once she had her on the run, the honey-colored

mare made sure Hotspot understood the lesson. She lunged after her, gave her a quick slashing bite on the rump, and chased her. When Hotspot tried to stop, the mare lowered her head in a herding motion and Hotspot kept moving. When she'd chased her half the distance to the girls, the lead mare stopped, circled back to the other mares, and herded them from the water.

"She's taking everybody home," Sam said.

Banking like a flock of birds, the wild horses swooped around the riders, but when Hotspot tried to follow, the lead mare charged her, driving her back.

"She's not allowed to go with them?" Pam asked.

"That's what it looks like," Sam said as the lead mare galloped after the others.

Alone, Hotspot circled at an uneasy trot. She was afraid to follow, but after a few seconds, she decided to chance it anyway, and swerved in the direction they'd gone.

The lead mare skidded to a stop.

"She must have eyes in the back of her head!" Pam said.

The mare swung her honey-brown head in a swirl of mane. She glared back over her shoulder. Hotspot halted and the herd moved on without her.

"Is she just, like, in 'time out' for misbehaving?" Pam asked.

Sam sighed as the Appaloosa wandered to the shoreline, sniffing the ground, and then, every few steps, raised her head to look after the others.

"I don't know, but if Ryan was here right now —" Sam stopped.

Was it the perfect time to recapture the mare, while she was feeling downcast and beaten? Or would she feel vulnerable without the herd and respond to any approach as danger?

"Let's catch her for him!" Pam crowed. "You've got a rope, right? Let's go!"

Pam's enthusiasm was contagious. Popcorn caught it before Sam did, and when he whirled toward the Appaloosa, Pam lost her balance. Her foot slipped from her left stirrup and her weight shifted. She was falling.

Ace bolted forward to block Popcorn. The albino squealed in surprise when Pam clung to the reins as if they were her lifeline. She dragged Popcorn's head down for a few seconds before throwing her weight back toward the saddle. She grabbed onto the saddle horn.

"Ease up on the reins," Sam said. She tried to sound calm, since Pam looked pretty scared.

"I almost fell." Pam panted, then seemed to hear herself and stopped. Finally, Sam's instructions sunk in and she loosened the reins. "Did I hurt him?"

"He's okay," Sam said, "but he was pretty surprised."

"That makes two of us," Pam said, and when Sam turned Ace toward Lost Canyon and the O'Malleys' camp, Pam only spared one glance back at the deserted lake.

"Mom, you won't believe what we saw!" Pam's eyes flashed excitement, worry, and disbelief. "These two mares—right? Mares?" Pam waited for Sam's nod. "Anyway, one's the lead mare and the other is Ryan's tame horse, you remember Ryan? Except she sure wasn't acting tame, and they fought."

"Are you both all right?" Dr. Mora asked as Pam dismounted carefully, then held Popcorn's reins in a tight fist.

"Sure," Pam said, meeting Sam's eyes. "It was just an adventure. A real Western adventure."

"That sounds exciting, and I'm glad you got to see it," Dr. Mora said. Then, as if the account reminded her of something else, she looked up at Sam, who was still astride Ace. "Do you want to get down for a minute, Sam? I'd like to talk with you about something."

"I need to get back, but I've got to put a lead line on Popcorn, and that'll take a minute," Sam said, dismounting and taking down the rope she'd brought for ponying Popcorn home. "So, uh, what did you need to talk about?"

If by some chance Dr. Mora had been watching the lake with binoculars, it was pretty obvious who she'd blame for Pam's slip.

"Nothing bad," Dr. Mora said as if Sam sounded like she had a guilty conscience, but then she asked,

"Do you think your Phantom Stallion fits the Dawn Runner legend?"

Sam had just clipped the rope to the halter Popcorn wore under his bridle. Her hands went still at the question and her mind glowed with an imagined Phantom, haloed with morning's first light.

"I don't know," Sam said, stroking Popcorn's neck as she thought about the question. "He's real, and sometimes he still acts like my horse, but lately he's been wilder than ever." Sam paused and Dr. Mora gave an encouraging nod. "When he comes and goes in the shadows, especially by moonlight, he seems magical, and my dad says he comes from a line of fast, light-colored horses that have lived on this range for a long time. So . . ." Sam shrugged. "I don't know. He could be part of the legend. Still, I've seen him more often at night."

Dr. Mora nodded. "You know, I've read that horses'—real horses'—eyesight is no different in darkness than it is in light. Something about the flexibility of their retina, I think. Their night vision is so perfect, they just carry on their normal lives—courting, mating, fighting, and eating."

"I believe that," Sam said, and a sudden sense of peace flowed through her as she remembered the dark hours she'd spent in the Phantom's secret valley. All through the night she'd heard the grinding of teeth, the gentle whinny of mares whose foals wandered out of reach, and the swish of water in a horse's belly as it walked away from the stream.

"I had my talk with MacArthur Ely today," Dr. Mora began.

"That's Jake's grandfather!" Sam said.

"He had lots of nice things to say about you," Dr. Mora admitted, but she was eager to discuss the legend. "It seems the Dawn Runner appears as a sign of good fortune. Capturing the Dawn Runner isn't the point at all. It's not an initiation like winning over a wild horse in manhood rituals and so on." Dr. Mora paused and pushed her glasses up her nose. "So, she'll probably only be a footnote in my paper. At least *this* paper."

Pam had remained quiet while her mother talked to Sam, but now she crossed her arms and said, "You're not getting ready to say it's time to go."

"Well yes, as a matter of fact, I am," Dr. Mora said with an understanding smile. "Since I have the information I came for and you girls have had your visit—"

"Mom, no. I can't go yet. I have to see what happens with Ryan and his horse," Pam insisted.

"But she's had enough of me," Sam joked.

"Sam!" Pam moaned. "I wish you could come home with me!"

"Next time," Sam promised, and something told her it really might happen. She hadn't forced this friendship to bloom again, but it had.

"Mom," Pam begged, "please."

"Tomorrow's Friday, and I could stay until . . ." Dr. Mora sucked in a breath and half closed her eyes, thinking. "Saturday afternoon. Yes, I could drive into Reno or Carson City and see what kind of horse artifacts they might have in the museums. But no longer."

"I guess that will do," Pam said, dragging her feet in mock misery as she handed Popcorn's lead rope up to Sam.

"I guess it will *have* to do," Dr. Mora replied in a tone that said she'd already been too lenient.

"See you at school tomorrow!" Pam yelled as Sam rode away. "And don't have any adventures without me!"

Because Popcorn was still skittish and unwilling to follow the shoreline of the desert lake, Sam took the long way home. She rode north over the foothills, following one of the trails that had given Mrs. Allen's property its original name of Deerpath Ranch.

"If anyone complains about me being late for dinner," Sam told Popcorn, "I'll just say it took less time than it would have if you had pulled loose and I'd had to chase all over the range trying to catch you."

When she finally came to a place where she could ride downhill safely, it meant threading through a maze of wind-twisted pinion pine that snagged at her bare arms.

"It's only like this for a few minutes," Sam told the horses.

There was a scuttling sound, probably quail, but the horses gave inquisitive snorts, because they couldn't see beyond the branches.

Sam heard the soft babble of water running over rocks. They weren't far from a small stream that forked off the La Charla River and ran behind the Blind Faith Mustang Sanctuary. The waters' whisper reminded her of something.

Sam concentrated, wondering what memory seemed important and just out of reach.

"Do you speak river?" Sam joked as she patted Ace's neck, but the gelding wasn't amused. His muscles gathered and he pulled at the bit as branches rustled nearby. "We're not running home," she scolded. Then she looked toward the sounds. "It's only the wind."

That would have made perfect sense, Sam thought, except that the evening was still. There wasn't a breath of wind, and something was moving closer.

"Let's go," Sam said.

She tightened her legs against the saddle, but when Ace stepped out, the lead rope snapped tight between her hand and Popcorn's halter.

"You can't both spook," Sam told the horses.

A twig broke with a pop so loud, it seemed to reverberate through her left elbow and Sam twisted to look.

Don't have any adventures without me, Pam had told her, and she'd planned to do as her friend had asked.

She'd really been more interested in Gram's front porch picnic dinner than anything else.

Until now.

Chapter Fourteen ❧

The Phantom's eyes looked black and playful as he peered past the frost-white ripples of his forelock. He stood close enough that Sam breathed the sweet grassy smell of him and saw the faint tinge of pink beneath the silver skin over his nose. She could have touched him, and her heart leaped up at the possibility.

She released her reins and was reaching her left hand toward the stallion, when Popcorn could no longer contain his terror.

Backing away from the stallion, Popcorn's hind quarters slammed into the thicket of pinion pine on the far side of the trail. Feeling attacked from all sides, Popcorn skittered forward. He lowered his muzzle and brushed an appeal for comfort against Sam's hand.

It was a mistake. Before, the stallion had ignored the albino gelding. Now he squealed in jealousy and half reared.

With lowered heads and clapping jaws, both Ace and Popcorn gave the stallion the respect he demanded, but the Phantom struck off downhill through the brush.

No! Sam wanted to cry out, to call him back, to yell in frustration, but she only whispered, "Zanzibar."

She didn't take her eyes from the shaking brush or the branches dragging over his silver hide, so she saw him stop.

"Zanzibar," she murmured once more, and the stallion looked back at her.

He whinnied and Sam caught her breath. That simply wasn't part of the Phantom's vocabulary. Like other stallions, he snorted questions and blew challenging jets of air through his nostrils at rivals to prove how tough he was. If that didn't work, he squealed in rage. And a few times, when he'd been totally content, she'd heard her horse whuffle a sigh through his lips.

But this whinny was reserved for young members of his herd who'd strayed and needed to be summoned back. She only remembered hearing it once. Now, though, it was for her.

Sam knew she shouldn't dismount in a desolate place so far from home. She shouldn't leave Ace and Popcorn tied to pinion pines at the side of the deer path. She shouldn't follow a wild stallion wherever he wanted to lead her, but she did.

The brush on both sides of the path narrowed. On each side, reaching branches clutched at her, and when she looked up, the gray-green leaves blended with the twilight. But the Phantom was just ahead of her, leading her on.

If this were a labyrinth in one of Dr. Mora's stories, she'd be afraid. She thought of Pegasus, born from Medusa's blood. And Kelpies, Poseidon's beautiful horses, crafty creatures that gladly carried any greedy man who leaped onto their backs, then galloped back into the sea and drowned them.

But the Phantom was no myth, and all at once, Sam knew where he was leading her. The lush scent of water twined with that of charred vegetation.

Suddenly, the hillside slanted beneath her boots. Sam walked sideways down the steep ground to keep from falling. An old barbed wire fence sagged before them. The stallion hopped over it and Sam lifted the latch, a loop of wire over a slumping fence post, and followed him.

When she looked past the stallion, Sam knew where she was.

The Phantom had led her to the stream at the foot of the drop-off on the boundary of Mrs. Allen's land.

During some ancient flood, the river had carved off a piece of land and left a steep plummet down to the riverbank.

As she watched, swallows stitched through the air, then slanted down from the plateau across the stream, dropping through the air to hover over the stream.

Sam remembered hoofprints in the sandy soil. She remembered thinking that by late summer, this arm of the river would dwindle into a stream. She remembered thinking Hotspot, who'd hesitated when she followed the Phantom's herd as they left the mustang sanctuary after the fire in June, would be able to cross it with ease by September.

The Phantom drank at the stream. Did he know he'd led her to the last place she'd seen Hotspot, until this week?

Eagerly, she looked around for the Appaloosa. She wasn't here, but that didn't mean she wouldn't come back.

Exiled from the herd, she might remember this place. The memory of food, water, and other horses could beckon her back.

For now, though, Sam was alone with the silver stallion. He stood in the shallows. Sunlight danced through the willow trees, reflected up in wavering patterns to paint him blue.

"Zanzibar," Sam said. It was the third time. She'd read that three was the number of times you had to repeat a magic spell to make it work.

The stallion came to her.

She held her breath as he nosed the scratches from the thickets she'd rushed through as she followed him. First he sniffed the cuts on her arms, and then his whiskers tickled her neck. She felt the stallion's teeth touch her hair and Sam flinched. She stayed still, though, when she realized he was grooming her like he would another horse.

The fresh, leathery smell of the stallion surrounded her. Sam closed her eyes.

This was magic, but it wasn't the bracelet on her wrist or a chanted spell that had drawn the stallion to her. It was friendship.

Friendship with a wild stallion meant happiness didn't last very long. For the hundredth time, Sam wondered if the Phantom could read her mind. The very instant she thought of grabbing a handful of mane and jumping onto his bare back, the stallion sidled away from her.

"C'mere, boy," she coaxed. "You know I won't hurt you."

The stallion's head tilted to one side. His forelock fell free and his eyes widened with a look that said she must be kidding. Clearly, the Phantom wasn't afraid of her. He simply wasn't going to stand around and wait for her attempt to ride him.

The Phantom trotted up the hillside, made a seesaw jump over the barbed wire fence, and then turned toward the pinion pines. Sam heard his shoulder graze dry twigs and crack them. Then, with a flick of his silver tail, the stallion vanished.

It took Sam a lot longer to trudge back up the hill and hike the path that returned her to Ace and Popcorn.

Sam wondered what kind of mood the geldings would be in. After all, she'd deserted them to follow the Phantom. If she'd been either one of them, she would've been mad.

Horses, it turned out, were different from people. If Popcorn was traumatized by the Phantom's charge, he was making a fine recovery. If Ace resented her disappearance with his old leader, he hid his jealousy well.

Left standing in the shade, the horses had contented themselves with munching dry grass and dozing. Neither of them had missed her. They proved it with their sluggish reluctance to leave the hillside and head for home.

The first thing Sam did when she got home was wolf down the fried chicken and potato salad Gram was just serving to the rest of the family. Even though she'd detoured into the world of wild horses, she wasn't nearly as late as she'd thought.

The second thing she did was phone Ryan. She'd been thinking about his reaction to his dad and about Hotspot's situation, and she'd decided she should tell him about the stream that bordered Mrs. Allen's ranch.

Sam was thankful Ryan picked up the phone, until he began talking and wouldn't stop.

"I've been thinking I should get Hotspot to come to me instead of going after her," he began. "I might take some of her things with me and put them where she could investigate. The bareback pad, a bridle with her hair on it, things like that. What do you think?"

"That might work," Sam said, surprised at Ryan's creativity. "And hey, I wanted to tell you—"

"Clearly, I don't have the transcendent relationship with her that you do with your wild stallion," Ryan went on, and Sam couldn't tell if he was being sarcastic. "But I've decided to take Dr. O'Malley's advice and become part of Hotspot's environment. I learned from Mrs. Allen, when I saw her yesterday— oh, by the way, I tried Sky Ranger's temperament in conjunction with Roman's and it was a total disaster—that the Phantom's herd winters near her wild horse sanctuary."

Sam rushed to tell him about the mare fight before he drew his next breath. "Ryan, I'm not sure she's still with the Phantom's herd. I saw her in a scuffle—"

"Horses can have scuffles?" Ryan asked, laughing.

"Well, no, not really. But it was a disagreement

and it involved kicking and biting and Hotspot being scolded until she left the other mares."

Ryan was quiet for a minute, then said, "Well, she may well return there anyway. Mrs. Allen said Hotspot was actually in her pastures shortly after the fire."

"Oh?" Sam said. It was all she could do not to tell Ryan that that was why she'd called, but she didn't.

Instead, she listened to him talk some more. "I'm getting myself outfitted tonight, so I can camp out. The Kenworthys are being quite helpful, supplying me with outdoor gear."

Sam shook her head. His gratitude for Jen's family was great. She was wondering what had happened to the old Ryan, when he added, in an undertone, "The equipment is quite old, really, and a bit musty, but it's serviceable."

"Have you ever camped before?" Sam asked.

Mrs. Coley had actually told Gram once that the Slocum twins had never even made their own beds.

"No, but how hard can it be? I have dehydrated food. I can boil water for tea and I'm bringing a book to read. That should substitute for patience, which, as a matter of fact, I'm running short of."

"What?" Sam asked. Had he just hinted he was getting impatient with her?

"Now, as much as I'd like to chat, Samantha," he said sternly, "I have Mocha saddled and I'm about ready to ride out. Would it please you if I had

Jennifer phone you up when Hotspot's back safe and sound? Shall I do that?"

"Well, yeah—"

"Splendid. I thought so. Good-bye."

Even though Ryan had hung up, Sam's ears were still ringing from his plans and pride. The old Ryan hadn't gone away at all. He was improving, but he was still there.

Chapter Fifteen ∾

On Saturday morning, Sam almost crept out the front door without Pam noticing. They'd thrown sleeping bags on the living room floor and watched videos until their eyes crossed with sleepiness.

Sam glanced at the grandfather clock. That had only been a few hours ago. The aroma of popcorn still scented the house, though she was pretty sure they'd picked up every kernel they'd spilled when one of the movies they were watching took an unexpected turn and they'd screamed and flinched and popcorn had cascaded all over the rug.

It was Pam's last day here, and that was what kept Sam from leaving without telling her. That, and the fact that Pam had held her by the shoulders and shaken her until she promised she wouldn't go out to spy on Ryan without her.

Sam squatted, and whispered, "Pam?"

When her friend didn't move, she touched Pam's arm. Nothing. She rocked her shoulder gently. Pam moved as if she were boneless, then opened one eye. "Huh?"

"I'm riding out to see how Ryan's doing. Do you want to come?"

In a flurry of thrashing restricted by the sleeping bag, Pam sat up and stared so wide-eyed at Sam, it was kind of scary.

"What time is it?" Pam mumbled.

"Five thirty."

Pam kept staring, but Sam wasn't sure her friend had heard her. She doubted she was really even seeing her.

"Five thirty in the morning," Sam added. "You said you wanted to ride out with me."

Pam blinked once, then tipped as if someone had yelled, "Timber!" Once she hit the floor, she mumbled something.

Sam thought it might have been "Tell me what happens," but she wasn't sure, and she didn't ask, because Pam had already fallen back asleep.

In the kitchen, Sam filled her canteen with water, then grabbed a slice of cold pizza and a plum and dropped them into a brown paper bag to tuck inside her saddlebag. She didn't plan to be long, but it had only been a couple of days since she'd warned Ryan about riding out unprepared. Besides, the idea of breakfast in the saddle, at sunrise, was irresistible.

Ace came to her eagerly, with long, head-bobbing strides. He was wet from rolling in the dewy pasture, but he welcomed the saddle and scratched his neck on the hitching rail as she drew the cinch snug.

A crow rasped a caw so raucous, Sam felt like shushing him. Swinging into the saddle, she glanced toward the barn roof, toward the enclosure Dark Sunshine shared with Tempest, toward the ten-acre pasture. Where was the crow calling from?

Blue Wings, Dad's Spanish Mustang, stood still and staring in the pasture and Sam followed his gaze toward the new bunkhouse, but it was empty and she saw no flicker of black feathers.

"Better to leave him behind, anyway," Sam told Ace. His ears flicked back to listen. "Not that I buy any superstitions about crows carrying bad luck."

She should ask Dr. Mora about that, Sam thought as she rode Ace across the bridge and into the morning.

Across the river and nearly to Mrs. Allen's ranch, Sam drew rein. She sipped water from her canteen and admired it all over again. Its sides were covered with rainbow flannel and its metal rim had dents from hundreds of hours of hanging on a horse. It was weird how moments of stillness usually made you appreciate stuff rather than dwell on anything that was wrong.

As Sam was eating the purple plum, trying not to drip juice on her jeans, saddle, or Ace's shiny mane, she heard the crow cawing again.

Sam looked overhead, but the gray sky looked empty.

"I know," she said, and pulled the pizza from her saddlebag. She ripped the crust from the slice, broke it in three pieces, and tossed it out on the desert floor.

A brown bird she couldn't identify dove for it a minute later, and his flock followed, but still no crow.

Okay, and she was trying to lure a bird that was an omen of bad luck to her. Why?

Sam tightened her legs against Ace, but he didn't step out. That one second of disobedience made her focus on a sound coming closer.

Hooves were galloping, accelerating, shaking the earth and air. Just as Sam gripped her reins, heart beating in surprise, the Phantom exploded past, brushing her leg, bumping Ace off balance.

"Where — ?" Sam gasped, but Ace's answer was to leap after the silver stallion that had been his leader.

Don't let him go.

Take control.

You know the right thing to do, her mind yelled, *so do it.*

She didn't. The thunder of hooves put her under their spell, and she couldn't resist joining the

Phantom's early morning run any more than Ace could.

Her hat flew back on its stampede string, yanking tight across her throat. Her hair and Ace's mane stung her face with lashing from winds made by two horses possessed by high spirits.

The Phantom raced just a horse length ahead. Muscles bunching, thrusting, stretching, he glowed pale silver.

He might have leaped right out of the sky, Sam thought, covered in a metallic cloak of moonlight.

The stallion was playing, romping with her and Ace as he couldn't with his herd. There, he had to rule. Here, with Ace and Sam, he could act like the young horse he was.

Sam tried to convince herself of that as the Phantom let Ace draw alongside.

The stallion didn't look at her—merely allowed his silver hide to brush her knee—but she couldn't stop the questions stampeding through her mind.

Could she catch a handful of mane and pull herself from Ace's saddle to the stallion's back? Trick riders did it. A "flying change," isn't that what they called it? Easing from the back of one galloping horse to another.

The Phantom's shoulder bumped Ace's again. Was it an invitation or did he just long to be close?

Sam glanced down. Rough dirt and rocks blurred between the speeding hooves. Ace and the stallion ran close together, but there was still room to fall.

Chicken, one voice in her brain taunted.

Don't force it, ordered another voice, the one that had lectured Ryan.

But he was her horse. He'd come to her. He'd carried her before. Why shouldn't she try to ride him again?

Both horses' ears were flattened. Was that just from the wind, whipping them back, or were they telling her this was not a good idea?

Sam sucked in a breath, transferred her reins to her right hand, and stretched the fingers of her left toward the stallion. If she could kick loose her left stirrup, grab onto his mane, and pull, wouldn't her right leg follow the stallion's momentum?

Thick threads of mane teased her fingertips and the gap between the two horses yawned wider as if the Phantom felt her touch.

Dawn Runner brings the sun, and seeing it is enough, Dr. Mora had said.

Am I absolutely insane? Sam wondered.

No! She didn't shout the word, but she might as well have. The stallion caught her quick move from the corners of his eyes and slowed. He ducked behind Ace, colliding with the gelding's hindquarters.

Off balance and still half poised to close a gap that had turned into thin air, Sam fell.

For one awful moment, it was just like the first fall. Plunging head over heels, she saw earth and sky in one brown-blue smear. But this time she hit the dirt rolling.

Even when she stopped, she felt like she was still tumbling. Slowly, the world stilled around her. She felt sand-sized rocks in her skinned palms, heard a cawing crow and retreating hooves.

She was shaken up, but when she inventoried each body part with slight movements, she knew her arms and legs weren't broken. She turned her head side to side. No sparks flashed before her eyes. No heavy feeling told her to stay down and wait for help.

But that sound meant something. Not that braying, annoying crowing, but the rhythmic pounding of hooves . . .

She leaped to her feet.

"Oh no," Sam moaned, because even as she scrambled up, she saw the two horses' forms growing smaller.

Ace was leaving her.

"I don't believe you!" Sam shouted after him.

To her amazement, the bay gelding slid to a stop, letting the Phantom run on. Ace threw his head skyward, and though she couldn't see his eyes from here, Sam knew he was rolling them as if to say, *I don't believe you!* Then, the gelding switched directions and headed home without her.

Sam groaned again. Just because she deserved to be deserted for putting all three of them in danger didn't make it easier to watch her saddle leathers flap like wings as Ace ran away.

"It's not like I wasn't going to go spy on Ryan anyway," Sam muttered, then added, "so shut up."

It was one thing to talk to your horse. Talking to yourself was a totally different thing and that thing was craziness.

She was sick of this. She was not destined to ride the Phantom ever again in her entire life. He was a wild horse. He was her friend. She didn't want him to be tame and carry her around in circles like a docile pony. She wasn't going to try to ride him, ever again, unless he pawed an invitation in the dust asking her to mount up.

Sam gave a forceful nod to underline her decision as she crossed onto Mrs. Allen's property.

She hoped it was too early for Mrs. Allen to be up, because she planned to creep across the ranch yard, duck through the fence, and cross the pasture that held the mustangs of the Blind Faith Mustang Sanctuary, then follow the path down to the riverbank where Ryan would be camping.

She felt kind of sneaky avoiding Mrs. Allen, but Sam had ripped the elbow out of her shirtsleeve and she was covered with dust she couldn't completely brush off. Her appearance would demand an explanation and she just wasn't up for it.

As she walked, she wondered how the Blind Faith sanctuary was doing financially. Mrs. Allen had used funds raised in the Superbowl of Horsemanship to build her arena, but it hadn't been finished. In fact, it had a long way to go. Now, it looked like little more than a big round pen.

Between caring for the horses and her grandson Gabe, Mrs. Allen probably hadn't had much time to spend on her art. Mrs. Allen's paintings of carnivorous plants creeped Sam out, but Mrs. Allen had told her, pretty sternly in fact, that those paintings paid the bills.

Sam knew Mrs. Allen had plenty of land. The wild horses were pastured on the hundreds of acres rolling from the La Charla River to the edge of wild horse country that had once been a cattle ranch.

Since he'd moved here, Linc Slocum had wanted to get his hands on Deerpath Ranch, but Mrs. Allen had refused to accept an offer that would have made her a millionaire. Sam hoped the stubborn old lady would keep resisting forever.

Sam might have thought Mrs. Allen's huge grassy pasture was empty, if she hadn't caught the silhouettes of grazing horses about half a mile away, and if Roman, the liver-chestnut gelding who ruled the captive herd, hadn't given a loud snort to let her know he was watching her.

Sam clucked her tongue at the gelding, not daring to speak, because so far she hadn't heard the yapping of Mrs. Allen's Boston bulldogs.

Once inside the pasture, Sam hurried toward the sagebrush slope she'd have to ascend on her wobbly legs.

She only encountered one mustang on her way there. Sam's determination to keep moving softened at the sight of Faith. The Medicine Hat filly was a lanky yearling now, and her palomino-pinto coloring had paled into a dozen shades, from ivory to golden candlelight.

"Hey baby," Sam greeted Faith and, totally unhampered by her blindness, the young horse flared her nostrils.

On small hooves that made it look like she approached on tiptoe, Faith stopped a few steps away from Sam, stretched her neck and her muzzle, and picked a weed from Sam's hair.

"How did you know that was there when I didn't?" Sam asked, but Faith had already turned away, chewing.

Smiling, Sam walked on, glad it was fairly light now, because the path that twisted down from the drop-off was narrow and steep.

The sudden scent of fried bacon made Sam's stomach growl. Was it coming from Mrs. Allen's kitchen or Ryan's camp?

A corkscrew of smoke just ahead made her think Ryan was actually cooking breakfast, and Sam navigated the narrow path, just wide enough for a single horse, more quickly.

Ryan had made camp close to the river, between two willow trees. Sam could see him reading a book with Mocha tethered nearby and something frying—

no, the closer she got, the clearer it became the meat was burning—in a skillet over a campfire.

Sam was about to shout for Ryan to save his breakfast, when she noticed the tension outlining every well-bred line of the Morgan mare.

Mocha was watching Hotspot wade across the river.

Chapter Sixteen ❧

Sam squatted on the path, trying to make herself invisible to the beautiful Appaloosa.

Early morning light sifted through the trees, pooling in a bright circle on Hotspot's back as if she really were the Dawn Runner, bringing daybreak.

Mocha nickered a greeting and Sam saw Ryan's shoulders move. Then his chest swelled as if he were holding his breath. Ryan was only pretending to read.

Amazing, Sam thought. He was actually taking her advice to let the mare come to him.

Ears alert, Hotspot waded across the river. Her bareback pad and bridle were spread out on the riverbank. Ryan had said he'd arrange them that way, to lure Hotspot, but Sam knew the horse had been drawn by something else.

Hotspot's hooves grated on the sandy river bottom. Ashore and just a few yards away from Ryan, the mare shook like a big brown-and-white dog.

Slowly, moving in millimeters, Ryan lowered his book to the ground beside him, unable to resist watching as Hotspot came to him. Placing her faintly striped hooves with great precision, she picked her way around her bareback pad and then her bridle.

Sam couldn't tell if the Appaloosa remembered her belongings, but it didn't matter if she did. She hadn't crossed the river to check them out; she'd crossed it for Ryan.

Sam swallowed against the lump in her throat, hoping Ryan understood the trust Hotspot was offering.

He waited until the mare nosed his hand, once, twice, then a third time with such energy, she lifted it a foot off the ground. When he rose and faced the mare, Sam couldn't tell if he was smiling. She couldn't hear exactly what his words were, either, but she knew they were sweet. And when Ryan ignored the restless, neighing Mocha to reach for the bridle on the ground, Sam knew exactly what he was going to do.

There'd be no roping, no nooses tightening around the mare's silky brown neck.

Ryan planned to test his horsemanship and Hotspot's trust. After months of running free, Hotspot was going home.

Sam sucked in a breath as Ryan easily bridled Hotspot. Then a slow-motion vault took Ryan onto the Appaloosa's back. For a second, Ryan's hands and face were buried in Hotspot's variegated mane, but he'd pushed upright when she bolted, splashing across the river.

The fence on the other side was closed. Sam remembered hooking the wire loop over the fence post herself, but Hotspot wasn't looking for the opening. She was running alongside the fence, leaving as she'd come in, Sam guessed, because suddenly the mare was running faster, spraying water in a white arc behind her, and then she gathered herself.

Oh, my gosh. Sam gasped. It was lucky Ryan had ridden jumpers, because Hotspot popped over the fence like a rabbit, and he stayed astride as if he'd been born to ride bareback Appaloosas in wild Western places.

Mocha neighed, begging them to come back, but a quick drumming of hooves told Sam and the Morgan mare that Hotspot and Ryan were gone.

She had to see Hotspot's homecoming at Gold Dust Ranch. More than that, Sam thought, turning to Mocha, she didn't want to miss the reunion of mare and foal.

"Hey pretty, pretty girl," Sam called to Mocha. "You can come with me, okay?"

Pointing at Sam with cupped ears that were the darkest possible brown, even darker than her gleaming coat, Mocha considered Sam. She rolled her eyes and swished her tail. She didn't look impressed by her new rider.

"Listen, I was there when Katie Sterling told Rachel all about you." Sam held her hand out for the mare to sniff. Even though she wanted to hurry, it was probably time well spent. She would not allow herself to be thrown twice in one day. That was for sure. "Katie said you went equally well under English and Western saddles."

Sam's eyes scanned Ryan's camp for tack. Of course Ryan had ridden Mocha with an English saddle. Why had she expected anything else?

"I could try riding you bareback," Sam mused, but then she remembered something else Katie Sterling had said about Mocha. *She likes to be in control.* Lifting the unfamiliar trappings from the ground, Sam turned to the horse. "Well so do I, beauty."

Mocha was everything Katie Sterling had promised the Slocums—smart, mannerly, and well trained. She was also fast, and Sam reached Gold Dust Ranch before Ryan did.

With one braid finished and the rest of her long, blond hair streaming down her back, Jen was on the porch of the foreman's house as Sam rode into the ranch yard.

"What's up?" Jen shouted. "I was looking out the window to see who was coming through the gate so early, and—"

"Can you push a button or something to get the gate to stay open?" Sam interrupted.

"Probably, but—"

"What is it, Sam?" Lila asked. Coming through the door behind Jen, she seemed to crackle with maternal intuition that something was wrong.

Jed was right behind her, pulling on his gray cowboy hat and frowning as he asked, "Ryan got himself in some scrape?"

"No, Ryan's got Hotspot. He's riding her home. I just beat him, but—"

"I'll take care of the gate," Lila said. "Jen, call up to the house and tell Helen what's going on. Maybe she can reach Linc in town."

"'*Course* his old man ain't here," Jed said. "Don't know where he was off to so early, either."

It took Sam a second to realize Jed was talking about Linc Slocum, and he was right. If Linc had been present to see Ryan's success, it would have been totally out of character.

"You girls take care of that horse," Jed said as Sam dismounted.

Jen gave her Dad a "Gee, we never would have thought of that" roll of her eyes, but she kept quiet and then tugged at Sam's arm, pulling her close so she could whisper.

"He's been worrying all morning about Hotspot and Princess Kitty."

"What do you mean?" Sam asked.

"Whether there will be conflict over Shy Boots," Jen said. "He even called the vet to see how to handle it."

Sam bit her lip hard. "What did Dr. Scott say?"

"Six of one, half dozen of the other," Jen quoted the vet. Then, before Sam could demand an explanation, she added, "He said they might share the baby nicely or fight to the death."

For a minute, Sam felt dizzy. "I don't know why Ryan isn't here yet," Sam snapped, as if that would make a difference.

Jen drew a deep breath and shook her head. They both knew even the best riders could have accidents. Hotspot hadn't been ridden for months.

While they waited, Jen helped her cool Mocha out. But Sam couldn't help listening, hard, for hoofbeats.

At the sound of a car, Sam and Jen turned. Gram's Buick was coming through the front gates and it was packed with people.

"It's like a clown car," Jen muttered, as Gram, Pam, Brynna, and Dr. Mora climbed out. "But I don't get it. What are they all doing here?"

"Oh, my gosh, you deserted me!" Pam called.

"I didn't!" Sam yelped.

"I know," Pam said, grinning. "But I called my mom to come get me, and right after she got there, your dad came in shouting that he'd seen Ryan riding his—let me get this right—'jugheaded Appy mare,' I think it was, and she was running like—" Pam stopped and squinted her eyes.

"Like 'a cat with her tail afire,'" Dr. Mora finished, and she and Brynna were laughing like old friends.

"Yeah, that's it," Pam agreed. "So we all came, except your dad. Can you believe it?"

"I can believe it," Sam said. She could imagine him saying he'd skip all the hoopla, or something like that, but she didn't have a chance to ask Brynna or Gram if she was right, because just then, a very tired Hotspot came through the front gates.

The mare's head was high, sniffing familiar smells, but she moved at a flatfooted walk and Sam's heart squeezed in her chest. Anything could happen now.

As he rode past, Ryan glowed with an elation Sam had never seen in him before. She knew he felt he'd earned this pride, and that was great. Even though Linc wasn't here, the others were calling out congratulations.

But Sam couldn't. Not now.

Ryan tightened his reins and Hotspot stopped beside Jen's dad.

"Good job, son," Jed said. "Now, what do you want to do about reuniting the mare with her colt?"

As if she knew what was coming, Princess Kitty gave a worried neigh from the small pasture she shared with Shy Boots. The colt didn't seem to notice. With forelegs spread wide, he concentrated on nibbling grass.

While Jed explained the vet's uncertainty to Ryan, Sam made fists of worry and impatience.

"Jen," Sam said. "What's going to happen?"

"I don't know." Jen shook her head, looking sadder for the horses than she was glad for Ryan.

Sam closed her eyes for a second, and in that flicker of darkness, she thought of a story.

It might be a Bible story she'd heard from Gram a long time ago. In it, two women both told a judge — was it Solomon? — that a child was theirs. Even after lots of questions, neither woman would change her story, and since they couldn't both have given birth to the baby, the judge said, "Fine, somebody go get a sword and I'll give you each half."

Of course one of the women said, "No, I was lying. Give the baby to her," and that was how the judge knew *she* was the real mother.

The story had always fascinated her, but maybe because she'd lost her own mother, Sam had never quite felt comfortable with it. Probably the judge had made the right decision, but what about the other mother? Did she love the baby, too?

Who was going to play Solomon for these horses? Or could they both be Shy Boots's mother?

"I don't think we can sneak Kitty outta there without creatin'—" Jed began.

"No more sneaking," Ryan said.

He slipped to the ground outside the small pasture and gave the Appaloosa a pat on her sweat-dark shoulder.

Suddenly, a joyous, squeaky neigh split the morning.

"He remembers his mama," Pam said.

Head stretched straight out, nose pointing at Hotspot, Shy Boots whinnied over and over again.

Princess Kitty's eyes widened and her attention fixed on Hotspot.

They'd known each other in Gold Dust's pastures, Sam thought, but today was different.

As if she'd just recognized her foal, Hotspot lifted her front hooves in a rear with Ryan still clinging to her reins.

"Let her go."

Sam didn't know who said it, maybe she did, but Ryan gave a firm nod of agreement, then turned the Appaloosa into the pasture and closed the gate.

Kitty made loud sniffing sounds, but she didn't interfere as Hotspot went to her foal and began nuzzling him nearly off his hooves. Kitty danced in place, her flaxen mane flowing around her, her neck shining with nervous sweat.

And then, maybe Boots was showing off for Hotspot or something, because he stepped away from the Appaloosa, lifted a hind leg, and tried to use the tip of one hoof to scratch his chin. He fell, and before he could rise, both mares stepped forward with ears flattened, fixing each other with narrowed eyes.

"Oh no," Jen whispered, and she shot a quick glance toward her own mother.

But it was Brynna who moved toward the corral

with deliberate steps. Sam felt Pam's fingertips sinking into her arm.

"Now, Brynna, let me handle this," Lila said. "You've got more than yourself to think about, and it could get a little rough."

And then, as if the drama was all too much for her, Hotspot shuddered, lowered herself to the ground, and started to roll in the soft green grass.

Princess Kitty and Shy Boots just watched, and when the Appaloosa lurched back onto her hooves, Boots lowered his head, raised his tail straight up, and bounded into a joyous run.

"What is that little scamp doing?" Gram asked, chuckling.

Shy Boots didn't go far at first. With rocking-horse moves, he circled the two mares, going ever faster until he blurred in a crazy dash.

His happiness was contagious. Both mares took after him, manes streaming, legs loping so they wouldn't overtake him.

It might be okay, Sam thought, but she kept her hands pressed tightly against her mouth.

As suddenly as the gallop had started, it stopped.

Pam and Jen both sighed as the mares fell to grazing on each side of the foal. When he lowered himself to the ground for a nap, Hotspot walked closer to Kitty.

"Just—" Ryan began, then broke off. "We can't let them be injured."

"'Course not," Jed said, but there was a certainty in his tone that made Sam think he believed the danger had passed.

Lila and Brynna didn't look so sure. Maybe it was because one was a mother and the other was about to be.

"I'm ready," Lila said quickly to Brynna.

But when Hotspot was within steps of Princess Kitty, she stopped. She reached her neck around to the base of her back, then, openmouthed, she glanced at Kitty and flicked her tail in irritation.

"She's just got an itch that needs scratchin'," Jed said.

"Indeed," Ryan said tightly.

Hotspot reached her neck out again, but her eyes rolled toward Kitty. Was she asking for a truce?

Princess Kitty must have thought so, because she sighed through loose lips and leaned her head toward the Appaloosa. Then, the sorrel's teeth grated gently on Hotspot's speckled back, easing the itch with teeth that could have drawn blood instead.

Sam sighed as the mares moved so they stood head to tail, grooming each other like sisters.

"And there was no need for deception," Ryan said, as if the idea were new to him.

"Sometimes human thought just complicates things," Dr. Mora mused.

Jen flushed and sucked in a breath. She looked proud of Ryan, and Sam guessed she had a reason to be.

Still, Sam's thoughts were far away from this Gold Dust corral.

She gazed east and yearned toward the Calico mountain range.

She was pretty sure she'd made the same kind of decision Ryan had. Instead of sneaking onto the Phantom's back, she'd taken the fall.

She needed the stallion's trust more than she needed a stolen ride.

When she did ride him again, she wanted it to be as if she were one of Dr. Mora's legendary creatures — a centaur, half human and half horse.

As clearly as if that bonding had already happened, Sam saw herself riding the Phantom again.

Her hands tangled in his mane. Her cheek lay against his warm neck. Blue sky arched overhead and her bare knees clutched the stallion's galloping muscles. Sagebrush spiced the air and they both breathed it in more deeply than ever before.

As the kaleidoscope of speed-streaked images faded and reality returned, Sam knew their gallop together would happen.

Today hadn't been the right day, but she knew it would come.

From
Phantom Stallion
∽ 22 ∾
WILD HONEY

Leather creaked as Samantha Forster swung onto her horse's back and tested the saddle's position. This was no time to make a mistake.

Dawn's golden shimmer still hovered beyond the peaks of the Calico Mountains and the two-story white ranch house stood silent, with only the kitchen light glowing, but Sam was ready to ride.

Her bay mustang Ace flicked his black-edged ears forward. When she didn't urge him ahead, his ears slanted sideways, then back. He snorted plumes of vapor into the September morning, just as eager to leave as Sam was.

"Now?" Sam asked.

She did her best to sound patient, though it wasn't

like she hadn't ridden in predawn darkness plenty of times before. But her stepmother Brynna stood barefoot on the front porch, making sure Sam didn't leave without permission.

At three thirty-six A.M., Sam had heard Tempest squeal. The filly was barely three months old and she was Sam's baby. Eyes half open, Sam had lurched out of bed as if a fishing hook had lodged in the center of her chest and her filly's cry was reeling her in. Sam had beaten Dad down the stairs but his whiplash voice had stopped her before she reached the front door.

"Samantha. You don't know what you're runnin' into."

Outside, Blaze, the ranch watchdog, was barking. He didn't sound ferocious, just watchful; but Sam knew Dad wouldn't take her translation of dog talk as a guarantee of safety.

"I'll look out the window first," she'd protested loudly.

Too loudly, it turned out. Her voice kind of echoed off Dad, who'd come downstairs, too.

Sam pushed back the curtains covering the window over the kitchen sink and stared toward Tempest's corral. Dad stood just inches behind Sam, but he let her look first.

Wow. If she'd been an instant later or even blinked as she stared out the window, Sam wouldn't have caught that glimpse of waving paleness. If she hadn't dreamed of the Phantom's moonlight visit almost every night, the saddle horses' neighing and Dark Sunshine's circling hoofbeats wouldn't have made her stare past Tempest's pasture to see the silver stallion dash up the hillside, away from civilization.

"Dad, did you see—"

"I saw him. Can't think of one good thing about him lurkin' around like that, either."

Sam had stared at her father in disbelief. Even though he'd seen the Phantom, too, Dad had actually snorted when she'd insisted she had to ride after the stallion. He'd forbidden her to leave until daybreak and he hadn't been nice about it. Her disappointment didn't affect him either.

"But, Dad . . . ," Sam had moaned as he'd turned away from her and started back to his bedroom.

"Quit your sighin', Samantha," he'd said. "I can feel the draft from here."

Then he'd continued back upstairs without another word, despite the excitement that kept their saddle horses neighing and restless all night long.

Sam had stayed downstairs. She wouldn't disobey Dad, but her mind kept planning her escape—as if she would.

There'd been no chance to sneak out, anyway.

Brynna, restless herself in her last months of pregnancy, had stayed up to study maps as big as beach blankets, which she'd spread out on the kitchen table.

Just the same, Sam had gotten dressed, then saddled Ace in the darkness, making sure the latigo strap that held the saddle in place lay flat and snug. She'd taken a stupid dive out of the saddle a few days ago. Since then, Ace seemed to be waiting for another mistake.

Like the one she kept picturing right now, Sam thought. She should not be imagining herself leaning low on Ace's neck, urging him into a rash and reckless gallop up the rise, along the ridge and after the Phantom.

She should be keeping her eyes focused on Brynna, who'd appointed herself clock boss.

"I don't know what you hope to accomplish," Brynna said, finally, pulling her robe a little closer.

"There must be a reason the Phantom was here," Sam explained. "He almost never crosses over to our side of the river. Please, can I go now?"

A rooster scratched the dirt noisily, then hopped to the henhouse roof, fluttered his feathers, and gave a rusty crow.

Sam looked pointedly toward the bird. Even the chickens knew it was time to get moving.

"Okay," Brynna surrendered. "Be careful."

"Always," Sam said.

Despite Brynna's skeptical groan, Sam reined Ace, her bay mustang, away from the porch. She'd barely thought of shifting forward when the gelding set off across the ranch yard at a speedy jog that threatened to break into a lope if she'd allow it.

"Not yet," Sam told her horse, and his smooth gait turned to a pouty, hammering trot.

Sam had already opened the gates in the old pasture. She angled Ace through the first one, then let out her reins, letting Ace lope over the short, crunchy grass of the shortcut while she looked up, toward the trail head.

Other horses called after them, crowding against their fences as Ace bounded through the second gate and up the trail that ran behind River Bend Ranch. It was steep and crowded with sagebrush at first.

"Careful," Sam told her horse as the path began weaving through granite boulders. The footing disappeared between bleached drifts of cheatgrass, then turned dusty and choked with dry brush. Each time their passing cracked a twig, it gave off the smell of summer's end.

As soon as Ace reached the ridge top, Sam glanced back over her shoulder. A toy house, miniature barn, two little bunkhouses, and a bridge made up the River Bend Ranch. She was leaving it behind and riding into wild horse country. Smiling.

She and Ace were following the Phantom. The silver stallion was roaming out of his home territory and Sam had to know why.

"We would have had a better chance of finding him if we'd started an hour ago," Sam grumbled to Ace.

As if he knew and was determined to make up for lost time, Ace thrust his tongue against his snaffle as Sam shortened her reins while she decided what to do next.

Which way should she turn? The ridgeline trail stretched twelve long miles and it was mostly used by wildlife. Last fall, a cougar had roved the length of it, using downhill paths to hunt near Three Ponies Ranch, River Bend Ranch, and Gold Dust Ranch. Early that summer, Sam had seen deer standing in the last snow patches on the ridge, taking refuge from biting insects that avoided the cold. Sam had also seen New Moon, the Phantom's night-black son, on this path, and once—now twice—the Phantom himself.

Left hand steady on her reins, Sam leaned out, sighting past Ace's front hooves. One good thing about waiting until sunrise was that she might be able to see the stallion's hoofprints and figure out which way he'd headed.

But it wasn't as easy as it sounded.

Sam knew the Phantom didn't travel right down the middle of a path unless he was being pursued. Instinct kept him walking alongside the trails, through mountain mahogany, pinion pine, and other desert groves that might hide him.

Sam scanned the dusty spots between grass and brush. She saw a few pebbles, ants busy against the coming cold of autumn, and lots of different shades of brown dirt.

"I'm no good at this," Sam muttered to Ace, but she didn't tell even her horse that she could use Jake Ely's help. Her friend Jake read tracks and other natural signs as easily as she read books.

Sam cued Ace to turn right. Tracks or not, she'd never known the Phantom to head for Gold Dust Ranch. Okay, once, a long time ago, but turning right made more sense. This way would take her toward Deerpath Ranch and Aspen Creek. She'd sighted wild horses in both those places where water and forage remained through late summer and fall.

Sam drew rein at Aspen Creek about an hour later. Birds asked warbling questions as they woke. The grove around her was hazy with pollen and all the prettier because this year no cougars stalked the area.

As she'd watched for horse tracks, Sam had remembered Jake's warnings from last year. She'd checked the ground for scrapes kicked up by cougars' hind feet and tree trunks gouged by big cats that used them as scratching posts. She'd seen neither, and now she could relax.

Gold leaves swirled on blue water in a whirlpool between rocks in the creek.

The sun had risen and though most of the tracks she'd seen belonged to mule deer, every now and then Sam had seen the V-bottomed pattern of a horse's hoof. Besides, it just made sense for the Phantom to stop here. If she were a horse, Sam thought, she'd spend the morning here under the yellow canopies of white-barked aspen trees.

As Ace drank, Sam watched the fallen leaves race between the river rocks. Like valiant little canoes, they followed currents and eddies, bound for the La Charla River.

A clear hoofprint was pressed deep into the mud a few yards downstream, but it looked bigger than the Phantom's.

"It probably just filled with water and oozed out," Sam reasoned to her horse, but Ace was busy drinking.

And then he startled and shied.

Creek water splashed up, spotting Sam's dusty boots. Muzzle dripping, Ace stared and she turned to follow his gaze.

She squinted downstream, trying to make out whatever he'd seen, some form camouflaged by the aspen grove's jumble of sunbeams and shadows.

Ace's ears pointed and his nostrils opened wide. She saw nothing and heard only water tumbling over rocks. And one thing she didn't smell was the meaty, dirty laundry smell of mountain lion.

What is it, boy? Sam wondered, but she didn't ask aloud, just gave her horse enough rein that he could investigate and take her closer.

It was probably just a deer. Ace was jumpy and excited this morning. But maybe she should unbuckle her saddlebags and grab her binoculars. After her best friend Jen's accident a couple weeks ago, Sam had decided to start carrying a few emergency supplies along with her.

Except, well, making the decision was about as far as she'd progressed in stashing stuff in her saddlebags. But she knew she'd tucked her binoculars inside the leather pouch.

What was . . . ? The sound must have been wind in the dry leaves, but no.

Ace's stare had shifted to the other side of the shallow creek. Whatever he was watching must have moved, because his head lifted. When a faint neigh rumbled from him as he gazed uphill, she knew it had to be another horse.

And then she saw it.

The mustang stood all alone. It wasn't the Phantom, but Sam recognized the wild horse just the same.

The color of dark honey, the Phantom's lead mare didn't move. She didn't answer Ace or make any other sound, but something in the horse's solitude and stance told Sam the mare was in pain.

She wouldn't cry out if she was hurt, Sam thought. A prey animal in distress—even a big one like a horse—would make an easy meal for a predator.

And it didn't take Sam long to come up with a cause for the mare's discomfort.

The fight with Hotspot, Sam thought, and she could see it all over again.

The Appaloosa mare had gone missing from Gold Dust Ranch, and had been running with the Phantom's herd. Feeling threatened by the lead mare, Hotspot had lunged with teeth exposed. When her bite had missed, Hotspot had wheeled and launched a double-hooved kick at the lead mare, this dark palomino now standing on the hillside. Sam imagined the echo of those striking hooves.

Wild horses avoided serious fights because instinct told them too much was at stake. An injured horse, unable to travel with the herd, was vulnerable. But Hotspot wasn't a mustang. She hadn't known the rules and risks of being wild.

The lead mare stood off-balance, as if she were trying to keep the weight off her right front leg. Sam would bet a closer look would show her that the mare was holding her hoof off the ground. But she didn't urge Ace closer. That could spook the lonely horse into hurting herself further.

Sam's mind spun. She had to think fast. How could she help the wild horse?

She was no vet, no biologist, not even very good at roping cows. If she got close enough to rope the mare, what then? Tie her and try to examine her legs? Even a tame horse's hooves could be dangerous, she had proof of that right before her eyes.

Had the mare been left behind? How unfair was that, Sam thought, a lead mare who couldn't lead had been abandoned by those she'd protected.

The mare was watching her.

If she didn't know better, Sam would think the mare was actually appealing to her for help. Of course that was impossible. If anything, the horse was considering Sam's power as a threat.

The best thing for the horse was to be with her herd, even if she couldn't lead.

Sam's mind circled back to the reason she was out here in the first place. Where was the Phantom?

"I'm trusting you to stay ground-tied," Sam told Ace, though a squirm of uneasiness passed through her. She tried to talk herself out of it.

Why should Ace go anywhere? He had food and water right here. He was a tried and tested cowpony. He'd be just fine.

Sam lifted the saddlebags from her saddle. Without looking inside, she faced the creek. What she had, she had. It would be a waste of time to paw through her saddlebags to see what paltry supplies she carried, before crossing the water.

She took a deep breath and unfastened her rope from her saddle, too. She widened the coil and slipped it over her head and one arm, wearing it across her chest like a bandolier. Lame as she was with a lariat, Sam took all the tools she had.

Aspen Creek was low, barely covering the creek bed and rocks, and it was narrow, maybe ten feet across.

Piece of cake, Sam thought as she sat, eased off

her boots and socks, then left them on the shore.

She took four steps before the cold registered on her skin and in her brain. Then, Sam gasped. The creek sent icicle jolts between her toes. She fought the urge to curl over and grab her feet with her warm hands. If she hadn't been holding her saddlebags, she might have done it.

Piece of cake? her mind screeched. Piece of ten-million-year-old permafrozen glacier, maybe.

What had she been thinking? On an early September morning when it was barely light she was wading across a creek that would be frozen soon. How dumb was that?

Except she knew what she had been thinking, and the loose logic of it still held. She was thinking the pretty mare who'd helped the Phantom rule his wild herd needed help. And no one else was here to give it.

Sam bit her lip and took another step. How could she keep walking? Maybe counting would help. In Spanish. That would focus her mind on something besides the arctic pain.

Uno, dos . . . Oh, why couldn't her feet just go numb?

Tres . . . But not totally numb.

Quatro. Oh watch out! Not so numb that she couldn't keep her balance.

Cinco . . . Crossing the creek was tricky. Her feet must sense the difference between sand and round,

rolling rocks, or she'd fall flat on her face and . . .
Seis . . . the huge splash would send the injured mare
running.

Two more clumsy steps took Sam ashore. She
tried not to pant like a dog from relief. But she only
had to try for a minute, because close up, the mare
took Sam's breath away.

Dark butterscotch with a creamy mane and tail,
the mare was muscular and beautiful. And what Sam
had thought before was true. The mare looked
directly into Sam's eyes.

The palomino's expression was so intelligent and
expectant, Sam had to choke back the urge to talk to
her. Wild things didn't croon sweet words to calm
each other, so Sam stayed silent, but it wasn't easy.

Although the mare's eyes took in the saddlebags
and rope in a glance, she didn't bolt. She stood still,
favoring that right front hoof, holding it such a slight
distance above the ground that Sam wasn't sure she
could even slip a piece of paper under it.

But Sam knew she wasn't mistaken. The muscles
of the mare's left front leg were bunched and shaking
as if they'd held the extra load for hours. Or days.

Sam knew she had to inspect the mare's injury if
she expected to help. She let her shoulders droop.
She took slow steps, moving closer until she was only
a few feet away. Without moving her head, Sam
lowered her eyes.

The mare's leg was swollen. Just above her hoof,

a fly buzzed around a black blend of crust and goo.

To get a better look at the wound, Sam bent her knees a fraction of an inch, then a full inch, watching the mare for reaction.

The wild horse did nothing until Ace squealed.

Sam had to look away from the mare.

Ace was all right, but he was staring upstream again, and suddenly Sam knew the honey-colored mare hadn't been abandoned after all.

Moving through a tunnel of branches laden with gold leaves, parting the pollen, shadows and sunlight, the Phantom came toward her, striding down the river like a king.

Read all the Phantom Stallion Books!

#1: The Wild One
Pb 0-06-441085-4

#2: Mustang Moon
Pb 0-06-441086-2

#3: Dark Sunshine
Pb 0-06-441087-0

#4: The Renegade
Pb 0-06-441088-9

#5: Free Again
Pb 0-06-441089-7

#6: The Challenger
Pb 0-06-441090-0

#7: Desert Dancer
Pb 0-06-053725-6

#8: Golden Ghost
Pb 0-06-053726-4

#9: Gift Horse
Pb 0-06-056157-2

#10: Red Feather Filly
Pb 0-06-056158-0

www.phantomstallion.com

#11: Untamed
Pb 0-06-056159-9

#12: Rain Dance
Pb 0-06-058313-4

#13: Heartbreak Bronco
Pb 0-06-058314-2

#14: Moonrise
Pb 0-06-058315-0

#15: Kidnapped Colt
Pb 0-06-058316-9

#16: The Wildest Heart
Pb 0-06-058317-7

#17: Mountain Mare
Pb 0-06-075845-7

#18: Firefly
Pb 0-06-075846-5

#19: Secret Star
Pb 0-06-075847-3

#20: Blue Wings
Pb 0-06-075848-1

HarperCollins*Children's*Books

www.phantomstallion.com